A mysterious prank brought them together for a sizzling-hot phone call . . .

"What's this about?" Christian "Kit" Fleming asked.

Now how should Sherry answer that? Oh, I'm just a nosy little ad exec who's dying to see who wrote your phone number on a twenty-dollar bill.

"Listen, Sherry, I'm very, very busy. I have meetings all day tomorrow, and I need to be prepared. If you could just speed this up, I'd be wildly grateful."

Those were the most words he'd said to her yet, and Sherry became uncomfortably aware that he had a very sexy phone voice. She cleared her throat. "Well, you see, I got a delivery tonight, and I didn't have anything smaller than a fifty, so the kid had to give me change."

"Uh-huh," he said, the grunt tinged with annoyance. "Fascinating."

"The twenty he gave me had some writing on it."

"Writing?"

"'For a good time, call Kit.' And of course, your phone number."

"What?"

"'For a good time, call Kit,'" Sherry repeated. "And your phone number."

He swore. Explosively. Loudly. Repeatedly. She even had to hold the receiver away from her head a little, just to keep her eardrum from throbbing.

"Tear it up."

"It's a twenty dollar bill!"

"That's got my name and number on it! Tear it up."

"Why don't you meet me at the Peking Delight in McLean in, say, twenty minutes? We can have a swap meet, so to speak."

"I don't have time for this," he complained. "I'm a very busy man, Ms. Whatever Your Name Is."

Sherry's curiosity died a quick death. She'd learned all she needed to know. Kit Fleming was a first-class jerk. "Fine. Personally, I don't give a hoot whether you get more annoying phone calls on your super-secret private line after I put this bill back into circulation."

"Wait, wait, wait! Twenty minutes?"

"Twenty minutes."

"How will I know who you are?"

Sherry blew out her lower lip. "I'll be the thirty-year-old masquerading as a teenager."

"Huh?"

"I'll be wearing a Penn State sweatshirt."

"A story that blends liberal doses of laughter with a few smiling tears. I highly recommend it."

—Connie Ramsdell, *Bookbug on the Web*

Trish Jensen Novels From Bell Bridge Books

The Harder They Fall

Stuck With You

Against His Will

Just This Once

Behind the Scenes

Send Me No Flowers

Phi Beta Bimbo

Nothing But Trouble

For a Good Time Call

by

Trish Jensen

Bell Bridge Books

This is a work of fiction. Names, characters, places and incidents are either the products of the author's imagination or are used fictitiously. Any resemblance to actual persons (living or dead), events or locations is entirely coincidental.

Bell Bridge Books
PO BOX 300921
Memphis, TN 38130
Print ISBN: 978-1-61194-210-1

Bell Bridge Books is an Imprint of BelleBooks, Inc.

Printed and bound in the United States of America.

A mass market edition of this book was published by Kensington Publishing Corp. in 1999 by Trish Jensen writing as Trish Graves.

We at BelleBooks enjoy hearing from readers.
Visit our websites – www.BelleBooks.com and www.BellBridgeBooks.com.

10 9 8 7 6 5 4 3 2 1

Cover design: Debra Dixon
Interior design: Hank Smith
Photo credits:
Man (manipulated) © Nyul @ Dreamstime.com

:Lgfc:01:

Dedication

To Suz, Cyndee, and Chip Graves—
I love you and I'm so proud
to be your little sister.

One

"And I-I-I-I-I will always love you-u-u—"

Sherry Spencer's mouth snapped shut when her doorbell rang, startling her into silence. She turned down her radio, then quickly waved a hand over the nail polish drying on bare toes, before hobbling to the door and opening it. She sure hoped she hadn't been singing so loudly that . . . By the horrified expression on Timmy Walton's face, she had her answer. He'd heard her.

Life wasn't fair. God had bestowed upon her a love of music, a gift for writing catchy jingles, and a set of vocal cords that could warp sheetrock. With a sigh, Sherry managed a rueful smile. "Hey, Timmy."

"More candy for you," the young delivery boy from Stella's Sweets said. "Didja land another big account, Ms. Spencer?"

"You can call me Sherry, Timmy," she said, taking the box from him. "And yep, the Dippity Diaper account is officially mine." Her mouth watered at the heavenly scent of the rich, dark confections. Gosh, she adored her boss, who knew too well her . . . healthy respect for chocolate. Who needed a personal life when there was chocolate in the world?

Timmy grinned. "Stella says you don't look old enough to be in high school, much less be an advertising bigwig."

Not unused to such observations—in fact, sick to death of such observations—Sherry swallowed a retort. After all, Stella and her shop were a godsend. Resisting the urge to rip open the box and gobble one or two sweets right there, she said, "Hold on," then hip-hopped to her coffee table and purse.

"Dang, all I have is a fifty, Timmy."

Timmy rolled his eyes, and pulled out a small wad of bills. "Stella always makes me carry extra change on deliveries to you."

It was endearing having a local candy shop owner who took such good care of her regulars, Sherry decided. Then again, Sherry was probably Stella's most regular regular. "Keep five," she said, then accepted the change.

She waved and shut the door, then wobbled back to the couch, trying to walk on her heels to save her pedicure.

Tossing the bills on the coffee table, Sherry reached for the box of chocolates, blessing her sainted boss. But scribbled words on the top bill—a twenty—caught her eye, and she picked it up instead. "'For a good time, call Kit,'" she read aloud, then took in the phone number, noticing that it had her own area code. "Now there's an advertising gimmick."

The handwriting was flowery. Was it Kit's handwriting? Or was it someone's idea of revenge on Kit? Should she call Kit and let her know someone was circulating her phone number on currency?

While she debated, Sherry opened the box of chocolates and popped one into her mouth, moaning as the delicious explosion of flavor invaded her senses.

At the very least she owed it to her fellow woman to inform her that someone was bandying her name about. Right? It wasn't just curiosity. She might be doing someone a favor. A big one.

Having done a darn fine job of justifying her action, Sherry picked up the phone and punched in the number. By the first ring she was having second thoughts. Maybe she should just—

"Yes?" a male voice barked gruffly.

Gulping, she said, "Um, yes, by any chance is Kit there?"

"Who's this?" he asked.

Now how should she answer that? *Oh, I'm just a nosy little ad exec who's dying to see who came up with Kit's advertising campaign.* "My name's Sherry," she said, deciding not to give him her last name. "I just have a couple of questions for her, and I'd appreciate—"

"For *her?* Is this some kind of joke?"

The incredulity in his voice made her sit up straighter. For the first time she considered the idea that Kit might not be a woman. Of course. Kit could also be the nickname of a man. She looked down at the bill . . . and started laughing. And once she started, she couldn't stop.

"What's so funny?" the man asked, sounding exasperated.

Sherry rubbed the back of her hand over her mouth, stifling her mirth. "Let me guess. You're Kit."

"This phone call is over."

"Don't hang up!" she said quickly. "You're really going to want to hear this."

The silence hummed across the phone line, but at least he didn't slam down the receiver. "You *are* Kit, aren't you? Because I'm only telling this to Kit."

There was another pause, and then he blew an exasperated breath. "Yes, I'm Kit. Did Rachel give you this number?"

"Who's Rachel?"

"My sister."

"Well now, I'm not so sure. Is Rachel in the habit of trying to fix you up?"

"Unfortunately," he said, but his voice softened perceptibly, and held a hint of a smile. "Listen, Ms.—"

"Sherry. Just Sherry."

"Listen, Sherry, I'm very, very busy. I have meetings all day tomorrow, and I need to be prepared. If you could just speed this up, I'd be wildly grateful."

Those were the most words he'd said to her yet, and Sherry became uncomfortably aware that he had a very sexy voice. She ran a finger under her collar and cleared her throat. "This will be short," she said.

"Good."

"Uh . . . before I tell you this, just remember not to shoot the messenger."

"Oh, boy," he muttered. "I take it I'm not going to like this."

"I sincerely doubt it."

He took a bracing breath, loud enough for her to hear. "Let's hear it."

Sherry quickly took the plunge. "Well, you see, I got a delivery tonight, and I didn't have anything smaller than a fifty, so the kid had to give me change."

"Uh-huh," he said, the grunt tinged with annoyance. "Fascinating."

"The twenty he gave me had some writing on it."

"Writing?"

"Yes, umm-hmm," she said, biting her cheek to keep from laughing. As she saw it, the situation was rather humorous. She just knew he wouldn't view it the same way.

"Well? What was on the bill? And if you answer, 'In God We Trust,' this conversation's over."

"'For a good time, call Kit.' And of course, your phone number."

"What?"

"'For a good time, call Kit,'" Sherry repeated. "And your phone number."

He swore. Explosively. Loudly. Repeatedly. She even had to hold the receiver away from her head a little, just to keep her eardrum from throbbing.

Once he'd sputtered to a halt, she said, "So, do you think it was Rachel?"

"No. But I have a good idea who it was." He cursed again. "Tear it up."

"Excuse me?"

"I said, tear the damn thing up."

"It's a twenty dollar bill!"

"That's got my name and number on it! Tear it up."

"Now look, Kit, twenty dollars may not be much to you, but I can eat for a week on that kind of money."

He swore again. At least, she thought it was a swear word. She'd never heard it before. "Give me your address. I'll send you a replacement."

"No offense, Kit old boy, but I don't know you from Adam. I'm not real certain I want you in possession of my address. Who knows what kind of nutcase you might be, considering some of your acquaintances?"

As she reached for another chocolate, Sherry was treated to a fresh round of swearing. She tsked. "Anyone ever tell you you have a real potty mouth?"

"Well, what the hell do you expect?" he practically shouted. "I want that bill destroyed."

"Where do you live?" she asked.

"Great Falls, why?"

Well, la-dee-da, she thought. She had her doubts about just how good a time Kit what's-his-name would be, but she didn't doubt he could afford to spend that time in style. "I'll tell you what," she said. "I was hungry for Chinese anyway. Why don't you meet me at the Peking Delight in McLean in, say, twenty minutes? We can have a swap meet, so to speak."

"I don't have time for this," he complained. "I'm a very busy man, Ms. Whatever Your Name Is."

Sherry's curiosity died a quick death. She'd learned all she needed to know. Kit was a first-class jerk. "Fine. Personally, I don't give a hoot whether this bill makes it back into circulation or not. And let's not forget that I would actually be doing you a favor, Mr. Very Busy Man. So long—"

"Wait, wait, wait!"

Sherry felt tremendous satisfaction at the panic in his voice. "Yes?" she said, studying her nails to emphasize her nonchalance.

"I'm sorry. Really. You just caught me at a bad time. Listen, I'd like to meet you. I'll even give you a reward."

Her hand dropped, as did her jaw. It took her a full ten seconds to get her vocal cords up and running. "A reward? Thanks, but no. I don't expect to get paid for doing a simple human kindness."

The silence from his end sounded thunderstruck to Sherry. Apparently the thought of doing something for nothing was foreign to him. And she wasn't exactly doing it for nothing, anyway. After all, the Peking Delight had the best Hunan chicken in the greater DC area.

"Twenty minutes?" he said after awhile.

"Twenty minutes."

"How will I know who you are?"

Sherry blew out her lower lip. "I'll be the thirty-year-old masquerading as a teenager."

"Huh?"

"I'll be wearing a Penn State sweatshirt."

Kit pulled his Mercedes into the parking lot of the strip mall where the Peking Delight was located, and yanked up the parking brake. He was still fuming. He had no doubt about who'd pulled this stunt on him, and if he hadn't wanted to avoid the woman so badly, he'd pay her a visit and ring her vindictive little neck.

How many of those bills had she put into circulation? How many more phone calls would he get like this last one?

He supposed he should be grateful to this Shelley, or Shirley, or whatever the hell her name was, but he couldn't quite manage it. She'd sounded too amused on the phone.

He climbed out of his car and looked around. No thirty-year-olds-masquerading-as-teenagers-wearing Penn-State-sweatshirts presented themselves. He checked his watch, then strode toward the door of the restaurant.

"Yoo-hoo, Kit!" a woman called to his left.

He jerked around, just as a young girl popped out of a burgundy Mazda. At first glance, he understood her strange description of herself. She did look to be in her late teens. She had dark, shoulder-length hair she'd pulled back in a ponytail, delicate, unlined features, and the bouncing gait of a high school senior.

She was indeed wearing a Penn State sweatshirt, atop a pair of holey jeans, and blue, high-top sneakers. She raised her arm and let a bill flap in the breeze. Her grin looked far too smug.

As she approached she checked out every inch of him, and Kit felt suddenly stuffy and uncomfortable in his suit. He hadn't even bothered to change after work, heading directly to his den to prepare for the following day's meetings.

She stopped in front of him, still smirking. "Let the good times roll," she said, her eyes flashing humor.

"How'd you know who I was?" he asked suspiciously, staring at those eyes. They were the deepest blue he'd ever seen, flecked with black the color of her hair and lashes.

Beautiful eyes. Bedroom eyes. They were the only clue that would place her age at closer to thirty than twenty. There was a wealth of intelligence in those eyes. They'd lived and learned. They'd also stolen his breath.

"You were the only angry creature stalking toward the restaurant at the moment," she said. "Call it an educated guess."

"You wouldn't be laughing if it were *your* name and number on that bill."

"Now, Kit, lighten up. You should feel flattered."

"Flattered! Like hell. That's a private number you've got there, known to approximately ten people at most."

"Eleven, now."

"And who knows how many more?"

Her eyes went round. "You think there are more of these floating around?"

"Who knows? You called first."

She grinned again, which irritated the hell out of Kit. "I'm glad you're finding this so amusing."

"Sorry," she said, smile unrepentantly in place.

"Yeah, well . . ." He fished his wallet from his breast pocket and pulled out a twenty. "Are you sure I can't offer a reward?"

That lowered the voltage on her smile. "No, thanks."

Kit held out the money. "Give."

He could tell by the wicked light in her eyes that she wasn't quite ready to let this sick joke come to its natural conclusion. But then with a reluctant little sigh, she handed over the offensive bill.

Kit looked down at it and breathed out a short, succinct expletive. He'd know that handwriting anywhere. He contemplated focusing his energies on planning the perfect revenge, but then decided Samantha wasn't worth the effort.

"Recognize the handwriting?" the girl asked him, leaning over his hands to look at the bill.

He stared down at the top of her head. Her hair gleamed and the scent of her shampoo wafted up to him. An unmistakable scent.

"'Irresistible,'" he murmured.

Her head came up. Fast. "Excuse me?"

"Your shampoo. 'Irresistible.'"

"Hey, that's right! That's the name of this stuff. How'd you know that?"

She sure was a pretty little thing. Too bad she was perkier than a cheerleader. Kit hated perky. Perky gave him a headache.

Not only that, but he wasn't about to tell this woman how he recognized her shampoo. She now knew his private number. "I once knew a woman who used that brand," he said vaguely.

"Really? Did she like it?" she asked, cocking her head a little.

"She used it. I suppose she must have liked it."

"What did she like about it?"

Kit thought that was a really odd question, but the girl seemed genuinely interested. "I have no idea. Why do you ask?"

She shrugged. "I'm in advertising. I've got a pitch meeting with the big shots of the company that makes the product tomorrow morning."

That news jolted through him, and he looked closely at the imp in front of him. Oh, no. This had to be Sherry Spencer. The young advertising whiz who had an appointment with him the next day.

He would have laughed at the irony, if he had a sense of humor left. Luckily, he'd lost his many years ago. "What do *you* like about it?"

Her hand came up to sweep back a few stray strands. She winked and nudged him with her elbow. "Between you and me, I don't care much for it. With my regular shampoo I only have to wash my hair every other day. With this stuff it's a daily chore. And whoever was dumb enough to name an egg-based shampoo 'Irresistible' must have been having a bad brain day." She finally paused long enough to take a breath. "But I always make it a point to try the products before I start to pitch an ad campaign."

Tomorrow morning's meeting was going to prove very interesting. He almost looked forward to it. Except for the fact that he'd have to put up with this woman-child bouncing her way through a presentation.

Well, with any luck a little of the bounce might bounce right on out of her as soon as she saw him again. "It must be difficult to come up with ads when you don't like the products."

She laughed, which did beautiful things to her features he'd rather not notice. "I'm in *advertising,* Kit. I can prevaricate with the best of them."

Kit could practically hear the trap slapping shut around her pretty little neck. "I see."

She peered up at him. "You don't smile much, do you, Kit?"

"I avoid it as much as possible."

"Yes, I see that." She glanced down at the bill in his hand, then back up at him. "I'm still wondering what that woman's idea of a good time was."

"Oh, that's an easy one," Kit answered, as he slowly started shredding the twenty. "Tormenting me."

"Christian Fleming is a hands-on sort, Sherry."

"So you've told me once or twenty times," Sherry answered her boss, Fred Simpson, as she packed up her briefcase.

Fred dropped into one of three matching green guest chairs in Sherry's office. "He likes to be involved in all aspects of the business. So if he has his own ideas about which direction he wants to take his ad blitz, you just smile and come up with it."

Sherry straightened and propped a fist on her hip. "Why are you sending me? From what I've seen, Bella Luna ads are the exact opposite of the kind I normally pitch. They're sexist, artsy and boring."

"You might do well not to mention that. He's the one who came up with the concept for this last campaign."

"Oh, I can see right off I'm going to love the guy."

"Be your usual charming self."

Sherry patted Fred's shoulder. "Leave everything to me."

On the drive to the Bella Luna offices in Reston, Sherry mentally went over her opening remarks, but her mind kept straying back to last night. That Kit was a real prize. A booby prize. *Good time, my fanny.* God, she'd never met anyone so full of no life. If he wasn't angry, he wasn't anything.

Not once had he cracked even the hint of a smile. The man obviously possessed all the personality of a rock.

Which was really too bad, considering he was a handsome hunk. He was six-two if he was an inch, broad in the shoulders and lean in the hips. He'd looked to be in his mid-thirties, but a very well-preserved mid-thirties, seeing as his expression never changed enough to give him character lines.

With his teak brown hair and hazel eyes, his square chin and superb cheekbones, he could easily model in some of her ads. As long as the ad didn't require the model to look like he was enjoying himself.

Sherry pulled a Mars bar out of her glove compartment and tore the wrapping with her teeth.

Why he'd taken up so much of her thoughts since she'd left him at the restaurant, Sherry couldn't figure. Maybe because she had a real weakness for wounded animals, and she didn't believe it was possible for a man to be that emotionless without having been wounded enough to erect such a thick wall.

Two minutes later she arrived at the Bella Luna offices. Impressed, she looked up at the brand-new, five-story facility. "Nice place. I think you can afford us."

She parked and entered the lobby. A security guard checked her name on a list, then gave her directions and buzzed her through locked doors that led to the elevators. Sherry shook her head. Was Christian Fleming worried someone would steal his bubble bath recipe?

She had to be checked through at two more locations on the way up to the fifth-floor suite of offices, so by the time Christian Fleming's secretary led her toward the meeting room, Sherry was just a tad annoyed by the man's overinflated sense of importance.

So she paused a moment at the outer doors to smooth her jacket and hair, and plaster a friendly smile into place. Finally she took a breath and nodded at the secretary, who opened the door with a decorum that made Sherry wonder if she were being ushered in for an audience with the Pope.

She stepped into the room, and noticed two things right away. First, the decor was extremely tasteful, in rose and varying shades of gray. Second, she was in trouble of Grand Canyon proportions.

Kit Fleming was seated on his throne at the far, far end of the conference table.

And he was smiling.

Two

Sherry kept her serene smile determinedly in place as Jim Forbes, V.P. of advertising for Bella Luna, stepped forward and shook her hand. What she wanted to do was throw her briefcase at the smirking man at the head of the conference table and run from the room. But she was a professional, and she wouldn't let a little thing like seeing her career flash before her eyes get her down.

The woman who wrote the note on that twenty dollar bill should be sued for false advertising. Kit Fleming was proving to be a very bad time.

How dare he not mention what he did for a living? How dare he bait her into talking about his stupid shampoo? How dare he look good enough to eat with a smirk on his face?

Sherry allowed herself to be introduced to the ten or so people attending the meeting. She didn't remember a single name, even though she always prided herself on remembering names. So why hadn't she put Kit and Fleming together last night to arrive at Christian Fleming, CEO of Bella Luna Industries, Inc.? Because he'd never told her his *last* name.

Finally Jim Forbes brought her to the man himself, who paused just long enough before standing and offering his hand to make Sherry want to kick him. His grin had faded to a half-smile, but it was still dazzling enough to make her heart pound. He had brilliant, even white teeth, and his eyes, looking more green than brown today, glowed with promises of . . . retribution.

"Ms. Spencer," he said, squeezing her hand. "It's a pleasure."

I'll just bet, Sherry thought. Suddenly she wished she hadn't blithely handed over that twenty to him last night. She'd love to whip it out right about now and start waving it under his nose.

"Mr. Fleming," she responded, squeezing right back. "Thank you for giving Simpson *&* Bailey a chance to help with your advertising needs."

He squeezed harder. "This is merely a brainstorming session, Ms. Spencer. No decision about ad agencies has been made yet."

Sherry met him knuckle-cruncher for knuckle-cruncher. "Well, I'm sure I'm going to have a real *good time* convincing you that Simpson & Bailey will be the best agency for you."

His eyes narrowed and whatever smirk had been playing around his mouth up and vanished. "Yes, well, let's get to it," he said, dropping her hand.

"Sounds terrific," she replied, resisting the urge to rub her aching knuckles. She moved around to the seat Jim Forbes pointed to, and sat down, dropping her briefcase to the floor beside her chair. Folding her hands like a good little girl, she raised her eyebrows at Kit Fleming and waited for him to make his opening move.

God, the man was gorgeous. Today he wore a charcoal gray suit, with a maroon and gray tie. A power tie. How appropriate. The man exuded power, even as he sat silently at the head of the table. And it wasn't just his seating position, either. There was a radiance about him, and an ease with which he sat, waiting for his subjects to get comfortable, that was rather sinfully sexy.

If he had even an ounce of personality, Sherry would immediately pitch the idea of him acting as spokesman in the ads. He had animal magnetism to spare.

"Well, Ms. Spencer?" the sexy oaf said.

Sherry jumped a little, realizing she'd been staring at him. "Oh, yes, of course." She laid her briefcase on the table and snapped it open while she began her spiel. Tossing aside her chocolate stash, she pulled out the stack of handouts she'd brought with her. She gave background information on her company, on herself; and name-dropped some of their more prestigious clients.

She walked around the table, passing out her résumé,

pointing out some of the highlights—a few of her most successful campaigns. Then she returned to her chair and kept silent while she gave them a chance to leaf through the handouts.

She kept her gaze on Jim Forbes, but her peripheral vision took in Kit Fleming's face as well. His dispassionate face. If her credentials impressed him, he was doing an award-winning performance of camouflaging it. He tossed aside the sheaf of papers and glanced up blandly. The toad.

She watched in fascination as Kit nodded to one of his underlings, who immediately poured him a glass of ice water. A raised eyebrow directed at another won him a danish from the platter of pastries sitting on the sideboard. A word growled into the phone had his secretary scrambling into the room within seconds to hand him a file folder. He was, if nothing else, a highly effective dictator.

Sherry swallowed her irritation and continued. "I've done some extensive research on your products"—that earned her what sounded like a barely concealed snort from the head of the table—"and your last ad campaign. And while I applaud the . . . aesthetic quality of your old ads, I think a fresh approach can gain us some market share."

Sherry started pacing back and forth behind her chair as she spoke, forgetting for the moment that she'd questioned the value of one of this company's shampoos a little over twelve hours ago. "It's been proven again and again that humor sells product. I think if we push Bella Luna cosmetics as sassy and sexy, we'll appeal to a broader range of today's females."

"Let me stop you right there," Kit interjected.

Sherry turned to him, her brows raised in question. "By all means."

"It's also been proven that sex sells."

"Yes, but—"

"That's what I want the Christmas push to be about. Sex. Good sex. Raw sex. Wild sex."

Sherry was getting a little warm around the collar. Just hearing the word sex pass from that man's hard lips was enough to raise the room temperature several degrees. "Well, of course we'd want to promote the sexy quality of your products, but—"

"Therefore," he continued as if she were nothing more than a seat cushion, "we're leaning toward hiring a big name to be our spokesperson."

"A big name," Sherry repeated stupidly. "Like whom?"

"Like Tiffany," Kit informed her.

"Tiffany," Sherry said faintly. She was only the highest paid model on five continents. "Excuse me, but are you speaking of print ads?"

"Print, television, the works."

"I see." She gripped the back of her chair. "Mr. Fleming, may I have a private word with you?"

He raised one brow elegantly, which thoroughly irritated her. "Whatever you have to say can be said right here, Ms. Spencer."

"All right." She took a breath. "Are you out of your mind?"

A collective gasp bounced around the room. Apparently questioning the CEO's sanity wasn't a very bright idea. The only person not staring at her as if he next expected to see her lying in a coffin was the big kahuna himself. His expression hadn't changed an iota.

"Not that I've noticed," he answered her. "What do you have against Tiffany?"

"I haven't got a thing against Tiffany," she retorted, "other than the fact that I'm not certain she has a full grasp of the English language." She tapped her index finger on the table. "The point here is to get Ms. Everyday America to want to use your health and beauty aids. You're not going to get them buying Bella face cream by smearing it over a cover model's perfect cheekbones. How many women are going to rush right out for your cosmetics when you've held up perfection as a woman's goal?"

"Isn't it?"

"Personal perfection, yes. Trying to get a woman to be the best *she* can be. But using Tiffany as a standard of beauty will only make women resent you."

"I disagree."

"You're wrong."

Another loud gasp. And this time Fleming did react. He stared at her as if she'd just spoken Swahili. Obviously, not too many people took it in their heads to disagree with the idiot. Sherry could practically see the account flying out the window on hummingbird wings.

"I see," he said finally, glancing at his watch. "Well, I have another meeting in five minutes. Thank you for coming, Ms. Spencer. I'll be in touch with your firm shortly with my decision."

And with that Christian Fleming stood and left the room.

Kit sat back and swung his legs onto his desk, stacking his hands behind his head. Closing his eyes, he tried to wipe out the image of Sherry Spencer, standing there telling him he was wrong.

If it had been anyone but her, he would have thrown the person out on his or her rump. Kit had been running this company since his thirty-first birthday, and for the last five years profits had steadily climbed. If there was one thing he felt totally confident about, it was his business decisions.

So why was he even waffling about this? And why couldn't he get Sherry Spencer out of his mind?

She was an unbelievably irritating, stubborn female, and yet he wanted her on this project with an intensity that baffled him. But on his terms. Kit liked being in control. In fact, he was passionate about it. He recognized the origin of his need to be in charge, and realized that in some ways it was a weakness. But he also knew that, in some ways, it was the reason for his success.

For that, at least, he could thank his foster parents.

His intercom buzzed. "Your sister's here, Kit."

"Send her in."

He dropped his feet to the ground and stood, a grin tugging at his lips. A moment later his sister floated into the room, looking fresh and lovely. It never ceased to amaze him that twins could look so utterly different. Rachel's eyes were the clear blue of the sky, and her hair was the natural blond of their nordic ancestors on their mother's side.

"Hello, darling," she said, moving behind his desk and raising on tiptoe to press a kiss to his cheek. Then she dabbed at the lipstick stain she'd left behind.

"Hi, sis. What brings you by?"

"I just wanted to give you a personal invitation to dinner tomorrow night. Jeff and I are having a small party."

His eyes narrowed as he gazed down on her perfectly guileless face. Though he'd only found her again two years ago after a decade of fruitless searching, they'd grown as close as if they'd been together their entire lives, and Kit could read her like a book. "How small a party are we talking here?"

She waved. "Just a few close friends."

"Who are you trying to fix me up with this time?"

"Christian Tyler Fleming! You have a suspicious mind."

"Rachel Brook Strand, you have a transparent mind."

She puffed out an indignant breath, which, of course, gave her motive away. "I don't have any idea what you're talking about."

"I thought that after the disaster with Samantha, you'd have learned your lesson. When are you going to stop trying to fix me up?"

She laid a hand on his cheek. "Once I've seen you happily married."

Kit shuddered. "Heaven forbid."

Shaking her head, she said, "I just know falling in love would do you a world of good. Look how happy I've been since marrying Jeff."

"You're the marrying kind, Rachel. I'm not."

"Bosh. We're twins."

"Who don't look alike, don't think alike, didn't even grow up alike."

Her eyes clouded with sorrow, which made Kit uncomfortable. He should have kept his mouth shut. He hated that she still felt guilty for lucking out in the adoption roulette they'd been tossed into, when their mother had felt forced to give them up. It wasn't Rachel's fault she'd been sent to the modern-day Waltons, while he'd wound up with a not-so-funny imitation of the Bundys.

He raked a hand through his hair. "I've seen firsthand what marriage can do to people, sis. They learn to hate each other, they take no greater pleasure than tearing each other apart. I'm not falling into that trap."

Her eyes misted. "The Howards were not a typical couple, you know."

"I know nothing of the kind," he retorted. Then, feeling the need to cheer her up, he sighed and said, "All right, I'll come tomorrow night."

"Wonderful!"

"But," he said, holding up a finger, "I bring my own date."

Rachel squealed her delight. "You have a new girlfriend! How wonderful!"

"No, I don't have a new girlfriend. She's a . . . colleague." In that instant, Kit realized who he meant to ask to act as his buffer between him and whatever single women his sister had decided to throw at him, and his heart panicked. When had he made the decision to ask Sherry Spencer out? One night in her company could well drive him crazy. She wasn't his type. She had too much energy, too much . . . personality.

He liked quiet, sophisticated, undemanding women. The kind he could walk away from without a backward glance. He had the feeling that the more he got to know Sherry Spencer, the more trouble she'd prove to be.

Rachel waved, a knowing smile on her lips. "Whatever. Eight o'clock, and don't be too fashionably late."

His intercom buzzed again, and Kit waved to his sister as she fluttered her fingers at him and left his office. Still slightly reeling from the decision he'd come to, he answered absently, "Yes?"

"Fred Simpson from Simpson & Bailey on line three."

Kit shook his head, and took a steadying breath. However bad this plan was, he meant to see it through.

He picked up the receiver and punched the blinking button. "Fred, I was just about to call you. I don't know if your associate has reported on our meeting this morning, but I have to tell you, I wasn't very impressed."

Now that was a lie. He'd been impressed by a lot of things about Sherry, not the least of which was her unmitigated nerve. Not the least of which was the way she walked in high heels. Not the least of which were her shapely legs, and the way she filled out a tailored suit. Not the least of which was the shrewd and intelligent light in her eyes, in sharp contrast to the rest of her face. His brain had splintered apart. That had to be the answer. Maybe he needed a vacation.

Abruptly he realized that Fred had spoken. "Excuse me?"

"I said, Sherry did report on the meeting, and I'm sorry it didn't work out between you two."

She'd reported she'd failed before he even had a chance to announce it? She must have a solid hold on her job. Anyone else would've waited for the axe to fall, all the while hoping for a miracle. "Yes, well, she and I *did* seem to have our differences in concept."

"I'm sorry. I have another ad exec I think will agree wholeheartedly with your vision, and I'd be happy to—"

"Who said I wanted another ad exec?"

"I was hoping I could convince you to use Simpson *&* Bailey just the same."

"I plan on using Simpson *&* Bailey." A shocked silence buzzed through the phone. "On one condition," he added. "Actually two. Nope, make that three."

"And they are?"

"One, I want Sherry Spencer to handle the account. Two, we can discuss concept again, but if she still doesn't convince me, she does it my way. And three, she's got exactly one chance to convince me. Tomorrow night over dinner."

Another stunned silence. "Well?" Kit said impatiently.

"Can you hold for a moment while I discuss this with Sherry?"

Normally Kit wouldn't languish on hold for anyone, but for

some reason this felt important enough to allow it. "Make it quick," he said, then punched the speaker button and dropped the phone into its cradle.

While he waited, Kit tried to read the latest quarterly report, but the numbers just weren't sinking in. He felt a strange agitation, and decided it was because he had the feeling Sherry Spencer would prove to be more trouble than she—or any woman for that matter—would be worth.

Several minutes later, the phone clicked again. Only this time it wasn't Fred on the line, but the woman in question herself.

"Mr. Fleming?" she said, her tone about fifty degrees below zero.

He picked up the phone. "Ms. Spencer."

"I'm pleased you're willing to hear me out again. I'd be happy to schedule a meeting in the next few days—"

"The meeting's scheduled, Ms. Spencer. Tomorrow night, eight o'clock."

"But—"

"I have a dinner engagement I have to attend tomorrow night, and I'm not looking forward to it very much. I was hoping I could put in an appearance and get our meeting out of the way, all in one shot"

Silence. Kit was fairly certain she was deciding whether to feel insulted or relieved. When she finally spoke, he could tell relief had won out. Which he found rather annoying. "All right, Kit my man, it's a deal."

"Fine."

"How should I dress?"

Some small demon grabbed Kit by the tail. "In something sheer?"

"In your dreams, Fleming."

Only this young woman would have the audacity to address him so familiarly. Which told him several unflattering things. One, she didn't consider him a physical or emotional threat. Two, she wasn't all that worried about losing the account. And one and two led him to observation number three. He did not have control over this lady.

Which made her dangerous.

Three

"Eat your heart out, Sharon Stone," Sherry murmured, as she tugged at the hem of her dress. She turned this way and that in front of the mirror, and her confidence collapsed.

Why should she care if Kit Fleming approved of her attire, anyway? As far as she was concerned, he'd forced her into going on this . . . outing to begin with. If she'd had her way, they'd have met in the safety of his office. How much business could they conduct at a dinner party, anyway?

She again looked in the mirror and surveyed her latest selection, a midnight blue, sleeveless number with a heart-shaped neckline. She supposed it would have to do. It appeared sophisticated enough, she figured, that people wouldn't think she was heading for the nearest prom.

Adding the diamond pendant necklace and matching earrings she'd treated herself to last Christmas, she checked herself out one last time. She'd swept her hair back in an artless bun, leaving a few strands free to tickle her bare shoulders. It looked all right, she decided.

His knock came as she slipped on her black patent leather pumps and her heart tripped up. Telling herself she was just nervous over changing Kit's mind about the ad concept, she headed for the entrance to her apartment.

She took one deep, cleansing breath and then opened the door. Her pulse pounded in her throat at the sight of him. The jerk was just too darn attractive for his own good. And he happened to look delectable in a navy blue Armani suit.

His eyes flickered over her once, before resting on her face. His facial muscles hadn't moved in the slightest. "You look like you're heading for the prom."

Well, now, that was *not* a good opening line. Sherry took one step backward and slammed the door in his impassive, arrogant, aggravating face.

There was a moment of silence, before he knocked again. Sherry stood with her arms folded over her chest.

"Sherry?" he said, from the other side of her door. "What did I say?"

She ignored him.

"All right, I'm sorry. I take it you don't get a kick out of looking younger than your age." He paused. "Most women would kill to look so young." He paused again. "I bet the rest of the women there tonight will be green with envy," he added, his voice coaxing and patronizing all at once.

"Or think you went cruising high schools to get yourself a date," she retorted, opening the door just as he was about to knock again.

He actually appeared chagrined. "Look, I'm sorry. You really look great. I'm sure your boyfriend would be jealous."

Sherry snorted. "Boyfriend? Let's see, the last time I had one of those, I think there was another president in the White House."

His eyes widened. "You're kidding!"

Astonishment! Another expression. Sherry felt rather victorious, and the night had barely begun. "I've been a real disappointment to my mother."

He really did look slightly stunned. Sherry decided to take that as a compliment. In actuality she'd had several dates over the last couple of years, but in every case she'd met the men at an agreed-upon destination, just so she wouldn't have to worry about inviting them in at the end of the night.

She hadn't had a serious relationship since college. She'd been too busy making a name for herself in her chosen profession, too busy to notice anything missing. She'd put her romantic heart in deep freeze, always assuming that when the right man came along, she'd know it.

She looked at Kit and her stomach clutched. No way. She didn't care how handsome the cuss was, his personality left a lot to be desired. She wanted someone she could laugh with, share her ups and downs, share dreams. The only thing worth sharing with Kit would be a—

Sherry almost burst out laughing at the scandalous train of her thoughts. She wondered how Kit would react if she told him she considered him good for only one thing. Well, actually two. He was also very adept at annoying her.

"Ready?" he inquired.

"Let me get my coat," she said, moving to her coat closet. He helped her don her black cashmere coat, and she had to suppress a shiver when his fingers brushed over her bare shoulder.

She turned to see if the sizzling contact could coax yet another expression from him, but his features were settled in an expressionless mask. She didn't care for the fact that she felt disappointed. "Ready."

The same sleek little Mercedes coupe he'd driven the other day awaited them in her parking lot. Sherry murmured her pleasure as the leather seat practically wrapped itself around her in luxurious comfort.

The car smelled brand-spanking new. While Kit rounded the hood on his way to the driver's side, Sherry admired the grace of his stride. Lord, she loved the way sexy men swaggered.

Okay, so she found him sexy. No problem. There were plenty of sexy men in the world. There had to be lots of them sexier than this one. She just couldn't think of one off the top of her head. And considering she spent so much time around models and commercial actors, that was saying plenty.

What it was saying, she didn't like hearing.

They accomplished most of the ride to his sister's Georgetown home in relative silence. Sherry tried once to bring up the subject of business, but he cut her off with a terse, "Later."

As they traversed the Key Bridge, Sherry crossed her legs, smoothing the skirt of her dress. When she glanced up, she realized that his eyes had strayed from the road to her gams.

He swallowed as he again focused straight ahead. "You look great tonight."

Thunderstruck, Sherry needed a moment to answer him. When she did, her "Thanks" came out a little croaky. She cleared her throat. "I hope I'm dressed appropriately for the occasion."

"Perfect."

He'd said it tonelessly, but still a little thrill chased up her spine. "What is the occasion, anyway?"

"My sister thinks she's found me another live one."

"Excuse me?"

"Remember my matchmaking sister?"

"Oh . . . oh, right. Well, if she's trying to fix you up, why are you showing up with a . . . another woman?"

"Because I'm not interested in being fixed up."

His profile was classically masculine, and Sherry really enjoyed the view. But then his words penetrated. "Now, wait a minute. Are you saying you're using me as some sort of decoy?"

"You got that right."

"Of all the . . ." She sputtered to a halt, because her outrage left her speechless. On the other hand, she wasn't certain outrage was appropriate. After all, he'd made it clear this wasn't a traditional date. Why should she care if he had ulterior motives for carting her to dinner, so long as he intended to let her talk business some time tonight?

Still, she felt an intense need to pop one of the miniature Three Musketeers hidden in her clutch purse into her mouth.

As they wended their way down busy M Street, he glanced at her. "You're not angry about that, are you? I mean, we can still conduct business."

In addition to being a handsome hunk, he was a mindreader, too. A man of many talents. She wondered how talented he'd be in—

Don't go there, she told herself, mimicking words she'd heard spoken over and over on talk shows. She wasn't exactly sure what the phrase meant, but a Sherry translation went something like, *Think about something else. Fast.*

"No, I suppose I'm not angry. I guess it must be irritating to have someone trying to hook you up all the time."

"My sister means well," he said, and his hard mouth softened a little.

Ah, he and his sister were close. Sherry thought that was sweet. "I always wished I had a little sister growing up," she said wistfully.

His mouth immediately tightened. Sherry replayed the words through her head, to figure out how such an innocuous sentiment could make him angry.

Not finding an answer, she continued, "I only have an older brother. He's great, but still, a sister would have been nice."

Kit didn't answer her, and she decided he wasn't interested in her life history. Moments later they pulled up to a wrought-iron gate, and Sherry had to keep herself from whistling her appreciation. In Georgetown, driveways leading to garages were rare luxuries. Circular driveways like the one she spied between the posts of the gate were practically nonexistent.

After parking, they strolled the short distance across the brick driveway, and Sherry stifled a gasp at the profound elegance of Kit's sister's home. It was a Georgian brick with white columns rising to a second-story wrap-around balcony. Sherry knew a sudden desire to start speaking with a Southern accent.

A huge front door again opened magically at their arrival. Kit's sister sure didn't believe in inconveniencing her guests.

A butler took her jacket and then she and Kit crossed the marble foyer toward the party sounds coming from a closed room to the right. As that door swung open, the music and laughter swelled, and they entered a large salon, filled with close to fifty people.

Between the five crystal chandeliers and the gowns of the women, the room literally glittered. Even the many palms in brass planters had small white lights encircling their fronds. A minimum of furniture had been backed up to the walls, leaving a large area free for people to roam and mingle. In the far left corner, a string quartet played chamber music.

"This is a cozy dinner party?" Sherry asked out of the side

of her mouth.

"My sister doesn't entertain for less than a couple of dozen people at a time. Believe me, this is a small gathering."

Just then a lovely blond woman broke from a group of guests and came gliding over, a delighted smile on her face. "Kit!" she said, stretching up to air kiss his cheek. "You made it before supper! This might be a first."

She turned curious but friendly blue eyes on Sherry and held out her hand. "Welcome. I'm Rachel Strand, Kit's sister."

This was Kit's sister? Could two siblings look less alike? Act less alike? While Kit walked around like an emotionless robot, his sister had an expressive, open face. "Sherry Spencer."

"Sherry. What a lovely name."

"Thank you."

"Kit tells me you're a colleague. How funny. You look more like a co-ed."

"Careful, sis," Kit said, dropping an overly familiar arm around Sherry's shoulders. His fingers traced little patterns on her suddenly sensitive skin. "Sherry's real touchy about not looking her age."

Rachel's laughter was musical, making it hard for Sherry to get irritated with her. Her lug of a brother, on the other hand, was taking liberties with her shoulder. If there weren't plenty of curious eyes on the three of them, Sherry would slap his hand away. As it was, she submitted to the too sensual caresses, making a mental note to give him a piece of her mind . . . later.

"You're blessed," Rachel said. "In a few years you'll be grateful. Trust this thirtysomething on that."

Sherry was about to inform Rachel she had also just joined the ranks of thirtysomethings, but abruptly Kit's hand stilled on her shoulder, and his body went stiff beside hers. She looked up, to find Kit glaring at something or someone in the room. Rachel blocked Sherry's view of the object of his wrath.

"Why didn't you tell me Samantha would be here?" Kit growled.

Samantha? Who was Samantha?

Rachel frowned, her eyes clouding a little. "I didn't have a choice, Kit. She managed to get Peter Neilson to bring her as his date."

"You could have told me. I wouldn't have come."

"That's why I didn't tell you."

Kit glared at his sister, but she just laughed. "You can't avoid her forever."

"I'd love to give it a shot."

"Don't be a baby." She waved at someone behind them. "Go get yourselves something to drink. I need to welcome the Stuarts."

"Where's Jeff?"

Rachel rolled her eyes. "Where else? Talking business in his den."

Rachel floated away, her filmy silver gown trailing in her wake.

"Do I need to know who Samantha is, and am I in danger of getting clawed by her any time soon?" Sherry asked, when Kit finally remembered she was there.

Amazingly, amazingly, amazingly, he smiled down at her. It wasn't the cat-circling-the-canary smile he'd bestowed on her yesterday morning, but a full-fledged baby-you-light-my-fire smile. The performance of a lifetime.

Who cared? It was a beautiful smile and she couldn't stop staring at it. Then to fluster her further, he lowered his head and brushed his lips over hers.

It was the briefest of kisses, but she felt it all the way down to her toes. Butterflies came to life in her stomach, nerves quivered in her legs.

Then reality doused her like a bucket of cold water. He was *using* her. He no more wanted to kiss her than he wanted to have a chat with that Samantha woman. This was all an act for him, and she'd been fool enough to react like a schoolgirl receiving her first kiss.

Sherry smiled up at him and batted her eyes coyly. He wasn't the only accomplished thespian in this crowd. Rolling up on tiptoe, she kissed him back. It was just as brief as his kiss, but because she'd initiated it, she'd had that split second to wrap some control around her body.

Letting her heels hit the gleaming wood floor, she said, still smiling like a woman in love, "Do that again and I will rip your heart out."

For a moment he looked utterly bamboozled, as he swallowed several times right in a row. Then the smile returned to his face and he brushed a strand of her hair back over her shoulder, making certain his fingertips grazed her skin again. "That might be a little tough, darlin'. I haven't got a heart."

"Now that's a shocker," she retorted through achingly upturned lips.

He chuckled. He actually out-and-out chuckled. The sound was a little rusty, and Sherry could tell right off that it wasn't a noise he made very often. Still, she felt the tiniest speck of pride that she'd gotten that much out of him.

"Well, well, well. What have we got here?" a woman purred. "The next notch on your bedpost, Christian?"

Kit's chuckle died quickly, and Sherry could feel his body go taut again. She looked from him to the woman who'd spoken. And nearly choked.

The woman was stunning. Worse, she towered over Sherry, making Sherry feel like an insignificant little elf. She had wispy auburn hair and deep green eyes and a perfect model's body squeezed into a black Chanel dress. Her nails were blood red to match her lips.

"Samantha," Kit said. "How . . . unfortunate to see you again."

Samantha laughed like he'd just paid her the highest compliment. "Aren't you going to introduce me to this . . . child?"

Sherry was not a happy camper. She tried to draw herself up to her full five feet five inches, but she still felt trivial in the scheme of things.

"Looks can be deceiving, Samantha," Kit said, his tone silky, "as I've learned well, recently." He squeezed Sherry's shoulder, whether for support or in warning, she didn't know. "Sherry Spencer, meet Samantha Richards. Sherry works for

Simpson *&* Bailey. She's just won the Bella Luna advertising account."

"Charmed," Samantha said, with all the sincerity of a snake oil salesman.

"Right back atcha," Sherry retorted, with as much earnestness.

Samantha barely glanced at her. She returned her attention to Kit, and the hunger in her eyes was almost unbearable to watch. "Mixing business and pleasure these days, Kit?"

Kit smiled down at Sherry as if he treasured every little atom in her body, then looked back at Samantha. "You know, it's funny, but we met before we knew we'd be working together. Want to hear how? It's a story of destiny."

"Oh, I'm all ears."

Sherry thought the woman was more boobs than ears, but decided not to point that out.

"We met through a twenty dollar bill," Kit said. "Sherry found one with my name and number on it, and she called to warn me. Wasn't that thoughtful of her?" He raised his hands in a gesture of helplessness. "Of course as soon as I laid eyes on her, I knew she was it."

Samantha was now the unhappy camper, which pleased Sherry no end. Warming to her role, she looped her arm around Kit's waist and squeezed, pressing her body to his. Kit Fleming might be a stoic egomaniac, but the man had a yummy, yummy body.

Kit grinned down at her again, and Sherry's heart bumped her ribs hard. Dispassionate, he was gorgeous. Smiling, he was breathtaking.

"So, I have to thank whoever wrote on that bill," Kit said.

"And what a good time he turned out to be, too," Sherry simpered.

Kit leaned down and kissed her again, this time lingering a whole lot longer over the task.

Sherry would kill him later. For now, she decided to enjoy the ride. His lips were warm and firm, and she didn't think kissing had ever felt this good. She could imagine how well he kissed when he was honestly attracted to a woman.

He lifted his head and stared down at her, and if Sherry didn't have eyewitness knowledge of what a sublime actor he could be when he wanted, she'd believe the passion and confusion she saw blazing in his eyes.

His gaze fixed on her lips, as if he'd never seen a pair before. Then his eyes lifted to meet hers, and he shook his head slightly.

At once they both realized they were in a room full of people. They broke apart as if they'd zapped each other. It took Sherry a good minute to get up the nerve to look around and gauge how many people had witnessed that kiss.

Just about everyone in the room, she realized, face flaming. Everyone except Samantha, the ten-foot sex kitten, who apparently didn't feel like sticking around to watch the lip lock. Sherry discovered an intense need for chocolate. Lots and lots of chocolate. "I . . . um, think I need to use the rest room. Fast."

Kit cleared his throat. "Down the back hallway. On the left."

"Thanks," she mumbled, starting to turn away.

"Sherry, wait," Kit said, wrapping his hand around her arm.

She looked down at his hand, then back to his face. That's when she noticed the slight stain of a blush on his bronze skin. Kit Fleming blushing? She wondered if the world was about to come to an end.

"What?" she asked, voice huskier than usual.

"Um . . . thank you."

"For what?"

"For being a good sport."

"That's me. Good sport Sherry."

"Can I get you a drink while you're freshening up?"

If she didn't know better, she'd think Kit was just a bit unnerved. But she supposed it stemmed more from putting on a peep show for a bunch of his friends than from the effect of the kiss. In fact, she felt certain that was also the reason her knees were shaky. Embarrassment, plain and simple.

"If there's champagne, I'd love a glass."

One of his eyebrows quirked. "Celebrating?"

She swallowed and tossed him a grin that said she didn't have a care in the world. That she wasn't completely stunned by the effects of his kiss. That her body wasn't quaking inside. "You betcha."

"Celebrating what?" he asked, his voice suspicious.

Oh, wouldn't she just like to see him swallow his tongue if she said something like, *Why, landing the CEO of a multimillion dollar corporation.* The turkey. He'd used her to push away an old girlfriend, and now he just wanted to forget what had happened.

She smiled sweetly. "Why, for successfully fooling your girlfriend, of course."

He looked so darn relieved, Sherry wanted to smack him. If he didn't watch it, her champagne was going to land directly on his egotistical head. As if she'd fall madly in love with him over one . . . well, two . . . um, three tepid kisses. Okay, maybe a tad warmer than tepid. Especially that third one. But since it was all an act, no big deal. She desperately needed chocolate.

"*Ex*-girlfriend," Kit emphasized, dropping his hand from her arm.

"I take it she's the one responsible for that message on my twenty?"

"Oh, yeah," he grunted, scowling and rubbing the back of his neck.

"Poor Kit," Sherry said, patting his arm.

"Poor Kit, why?" he asked, folding his arms over his broad chest.

Sherry shook her head. "It must be rough being so irresistible to women."

His gaze dropped to her lips, and a lazy, cocky quirk pulled at his mouth. "It has its moments."

"Don't flatter yourself, Fleming," Sherry retorted, turning smartly. But as she marched from his insufferable presence, pursing her still tingling lips, Sherry suddenly understood what Samantha had meant about Kit being a good time. He did, indeed, have his moments.

Four

Kit decided he might have to kill his sister. What the hell had she been thinking, seating Sherry clear at the other end of the table? And beside that lech Walter Haines, to boot?

To compound her sins, Rachel had placed him between Debra French, a notoriously man-hungry divorcée, and Samantha.

The only reason he'd agreed to come to this dinner party was the idea of talking to Sherry during and between all seven courses. For some reason he enjoyed interacting with her. She was smart and sassy and he liked the way her mind worked. Had he known Rachel would arrange them this way, he'd have done what he did at every other one of her dinner parties: show up after dinner.

"You seem preoccupied tonight, darling," Samantha purred.

"I am not your darling, Samantha," he ground out. "Especially not after you pulled that stunt with the twenty dollar bill."

"Oh, that was just a little joke, Kit."

"I'm not laughing." He glared at her. What had he ever seen in this woman? Sure, she was beautiful. Physically, at any rate. But the beauty didn't reach down into the depths of her soul. When she smiled, a light didn't come on in her eyes like it did when Sherry—

He squelched that observation in mid-thought. "How the hell many of those bills are out there, Samantha?"

She shrugged one shoulder. "Just one, darling. And it's the least you deserve after the way you treated me." She wet her lips. "But I'm willing to forgive you." She leaned toward him and whispered in his ear. "We can go back and capture the magic all over again."

Kit refrained from rolling his eyes. He didn't understand Samantha. After all, things between them had been fine and uncomplicated, and then she'd started getting possessive, something he'd told her from the first was a no-no. And when he'd tried to cool down the affair, she'd decided to spite him by showing up at a party with another man.

Unfortunately for her, he hadn't been the least upset. Only wildly relieved. Unfortunately for him, she hadn't been pleased with his reaction. So maybe it *had* been a little callous to slap her new boy-toy on the shoulder and offer his heartiest congratulations, but what the hell, he'd been caught up in the moment.

He looked at her, and not a single hormone stirred inside him. Yet, he had to tread carefully. Samantha had already proven she had a vindictive streak a mile long. And though he was still seethingly angry, he had enough sense not to tell her exactly what he thought of her and her proposition.

Grabbing hold of the first excuse he could think of, he forced himself to smile at her. "As tempting as that sounds, I'm afraid Sherry's a little jealous. I don't think she'd take kindly to us resuming our relationship."

Fury burned in her eyes, but she kept a smile on her face. "Whatever do you see in that . . . that child?"

"I assure you," he said, for some odd reason, angry on Sherry's behalf, "Sherry's no child. She's all woman, and all that I can handle at the moment."

Kit was saved from continuing the farce when the soup arrived. Pretending intense interest in the chowder, he picked up his soup spoon, then glanced Sherry's way. His eyes narrowed as he watched Walter whisper something in her ear. Her eyebrows shot up, and she sat back and stared at the man, and then burst into what looked like laughing disbelief. Whatever Walter had said to her, she'd apparently decided that he'd been kidding.

Kit knew better.

"Excuse me," he said to the group in general, interrupting Debra French's discourse on whether Frederick's of Hollywood or Victoria's Secret produced the better teddy. He dropped his napkin on his chair and stalked to the other end of the table. Ignoring a sea of astonished faces, he yanked back Sherry's chair and hauled her to her feet.

She emitted a small squeal, which he also ignored. "Please excuse us for a moment. Sugarplum and I need to talk privately."

Sherry was literally gaping at him as he dragged her out of the dining room, across the foyer to the small library. The windows rattled a little from the force with which he slammed shut the door.

"What the heck is the matter with you?" she demanded, plunking her hands on her hips. The action managed to stretch the material of her blue dress tighter across her breasts, which in turn made his mouth go dry.

She had to have the most beautiful skin he'd ever seen, and all he wanted to do was bury his head between her breasts and inhale it, taste it, touch it.

He wasn't surprised by his attraction to her. He loved women. He loved making love to them. And when they were as alluring as Sherry, he usually did find himself sexually attracted to them. So, finding himself getting hard just looking at her didn't astound him. What astounded him was that he was angry, too. But he couldn't remember why. He grasped her shoulders and pulled her to him, forgetting his anger for a moment and concentrating on the wanting.

"Kit, what the—" was as much as she got out before he covered her mouth with his own. She went stiff, and at first resisted his attempts to get her to open her lips and let him inside. But Kit was nothing if not persistent. He raised his hands to her face and tilted her head a little to approach at a better angle.

She tasted like heaven and smelled even better. He recognized the perfume she wore as Destiny, his favorite Bella Luna fragrance. It suited her perfectly. It was a bold, spicy scent with just an underlying hint of powdery innocence. Just like the woman. Although her face was all pretty innocence, inside she had the determination of a bulldog.

She started to return the kiss, and Kit felt his control slipping. He wanted her with a force that stunned him. Touching his tongue to her lower lip, he groaned when she gave him entrance to that delectable mouth. She tasted of wine and woman and . . . chocolate? God, her mouth was so soft and pliant, his brain fizzled out. His hands glided up her back to her shoulder blades and he pulled her even closer against him. Unfortunately, her hands were still on his chest, and prevented her breasts from crushing against his ribs. He tore his mouth from hers and kissed his way across her face to her neck and ear.

She gasped as his tongue traced its soft shell. "Kit, stop."

"I don't want to," he rasped.

Her hands pushed at his chest. "Kit, stop this. Right this minute."

"This minute. That gives me fifty-nine more seconds."

"Right this very second!"

He let her go. He wasn't happy about it, but he let her go anyway. Forking a hand through his hair, he tried to put a bland expression on his face, but he thought his heavy breathing might give him away just the same.

What had gotten into him?

"What's gotten into you?" Sherry asked, and when he finally found the nerve to look at her, he was happy to see that her eyes were soft with unleashed passion. Her mouth, that luscious mouth, was moist and swollen and he wanted it all over his body.

He threw out his hands. "Just playing the part."

Sherry made a show of turning three hundred and sixty degrees, which gave him a view from every angle, and every angle looked perfect to him. When she finally faced him again, she said, her eyes now twinkling, "Don't look now, but there's no one here to applaud your performance."

He wanted to ask whether she'd give him a standing ovation, but was a little too apprehensive about what her answer would be. That was the most spectacular kiss of his life, but who could say where it ranked on her scale?

"I believe in practicing?" he said, pretty sure it sounded as lame to her as it did to him, but the honest answer wouldn't do just yet. If he mentioned that he fully planned on sleeping with her someday—someday soon, he hoped—he had the feeling she might just take offense.

Some women were real touchy that way. They didn't want the inevitable spelled out for them. They wanted to hide behind restraint and respectability right up to the moment he carried them to the bedroom.

Although Sherry seemed like the open and honest sort, he wasn't going to risk blowing his chance with her completely by revealing all his cards. He'd gone as far as he had in his career by perfecting his timing. Now was not the moment to announce to this woman that she was his next acquisition.

He'd been right. The quirk to her lips told him she considered that a really dumb excuse. "Why were you angry out there?" she asked. "You looked like you wanted to shoot me."

"Not you, that jerk sitting beside you. Just wanted to save you from him."

Her mouth dropped open. "*Save* me from him? What in the world gave you the idea I needed rescuing?"

"I just know him. He considers himself a lady-killer."

"Walter?" She laughed. "The man is a flirt, but he's perfectly harmless."

Obviously the woman didn't recognize an attempt to pick her up when she saw one. Poor thing. While he had her in his care he'd have to watch out for her.

"How are you and Samantha getting along down there?" she asked.

Kit grimaced. "God, I can't believe Rachel seated us together. She's going to hear about it later."

"Your sister wasn't responsible. She whispered her apologies and told me someone had messed with the seating arrangement."

"Well, guess who."

"Right. I saw good old Sam in the dining room on my way to freshen up, but at the time I didn't pay her any mind. I just assumed she was pilfering the silver or something."

Kit laughed. Her jaw dropped again. Kit stopped laughing.

"What?"

"You know, that's the first time I've ever heard a genuine laugh out of you. I didn't think you were capable of it."

Kit took offense, even if he knew she was right. He'd had his sense of humor wrung out of him a long, long time ago. But at the moment, he sort of mourned its loss. Sharing laughter with Sherry Spencer appealed to him on some strange level.

Sharing a lot of things with Sherry appealed to him. Like a bed. Kit shook his head. Wrong place, wrong time. "I guess we should get back to the meal. We've probably missed a course or two already."

Sherry was not amused. She slammed into her apartment, three hours later, and headed straight for her pantry and her chocolate fix.

She'd had to put up with a lot of crap tonight, including Samantha Richards and her not-so-veiled insinuations. Apparently good old Sam felt certain that she'd get Kit back in time, just as soon as he realized what he was missing. And Sam had made it clear that Sherry was just the right person for the job of helping Kit make comparisons, so he could come racing back to Sam.

By the time they'd left the party—two long hours after the end of the meal—Sherry had wanted to murder Kit for placing her in such an awkward position, then abandoning her to the likes of Samantha Richards, while he mingled with the boys.

The worst of it was, they hadn't talked business once. Even on the long ride home, Kit had professed to being too tired to think clearly. She'd wanted to shriek at him. After all, he'd told her this would be her only chance to persuade him to change his mind about Tiffany, then he'd made it impossible for her to try.

At the door to her condo he'd imperiously told her to contact his secretary and make an appointment for a lunch meeting to discuss the campaign. She'd wanted to tell him to take a long walk off a short pier, but she'd bitten her tongue, stuck her nose in the air, and marched into her building, never looking back.

Kit hadn't even tried to kiss her good night.

Why should he? He hadn't had any old girlfriends hanging around. Of course, he hadn't had any old girlfriends in the library, either, but he'd kissed her there, too. Really kissed her. Like she'd never been kissed before. The lout.

After climbing into bed, but before sleep overtook her, she found herself humming a rather loud, off-key rendition of "Your Cheatin' Heart."

"Why haven't you called my secretary?" Kit asked, his voice vibrating with annoyance.

Sherry shoved her computer keyboard back under her desk and shifted the phone receiver to her other ear. Grabbing a bag of M&M's from her drawer, she said, "I've been busy."

It had only been three days since the disastrous dinner party, after all. It wasn't as if she'd waited a month. Of course, she had intentionally not called, but he didn't have to know that. If Kit Fleming thought her life revolved around Bella Luna, he had another think coming. If he thought he could order her around, he was in for a rude awakening. Sherry had a solid reputation and plenty of clients. She had plaques lining her walls, awards on her bookshelves.

He was lucky to have her, although the silence screaming at her over the phone line told her he didn't feel especially lucky to have her at the moment. She could almost picture him counting to ten.

"Lunch tomorrow," he finally commanded. "One o'clock. Clyde's."

"No can do, Kit old boy. I've got a date." With another client, but he didn't have to know that either.

"Ms. Spencer," he said in a soft, dangerous voice, "I think we've forgotten who the client is in this relationship."

"We have? No, I don't think so. What we've forgotten here is that we are not the only client this agency has. But, if you are dead set on meeting tomorrow, how about I patch you through to Charlie Weis, and see if he can't do lunch?"

"How about if you patch me through to Fred Simpson and I tell him what an insolent little account exec you are?"

"Okey-doke," Sherry said, putting him on hold, then forwarding his call to Fred's secretary.

She popped about ten M&M's into her mouth, then calmly went back to typing up some ideas for a diaper commercial. Really, some men just didn't get it.

It took Fred exactly ninety seconds to make it down the hall to her office. "What do you think you're doing?"

"Trying to come up with an innovative way of showing how Dippity Diapers can hold up to a gallon of water. Why, I don't know. I mean, if these were diapers for elephants I might understand, but how many human babies do you know—"

"You know what I'm talking about."

Sherry sighed and munched a few more M&M's. "The man is a dictator. I don't work well with dictators."

"Are you intentionally trying to lose this account?"

"Of course not." Sherry saved her file before turning back to Fred. "Kit Fleming wants a yes man to rubberstamp his ideas. I can't do it. Assign Charlie. He's real good at saying yes to everything."

"Fleming doesn't want Charlie. He wants you."

Sherry glanced up. "Still? Even after . . . that?" she said, waving at the phone.

"Even after that. He spent some time shouting about what a rude, unconventional, pain in the butt you are, and that if we want to keep this account, you'd better haul your fanny to lunch tomorrow, and you'd better not be late."

"I have another lunch date."

"Sherry . . ."

"With the Dippity Diaper people."

"Oh." Fred shuffled his feet. "Well, what do you suggest we do?"

"Send Charlie."

"He told me in no uncertain terms that's it's you or nobody."

Sherry growled. Apparently Kit Fleming was intent on tormenting her. Or conquering her. She had no intention of being conquered. "I'll take care of it."

"How?"

"Just trust me, Fred."

Fred looked uncertain, but then he grimaced, shrugged, and left.

Flipping angrily through her Rolodex, Sherry found the number and punched it in with a vengeance. It was time Kit Fleming learned he couldn't control her. When she finally got through to his secretary, she demanded to speak to the overbearing clod, but apparently Kit had left instructions that she run everything through his assistant.

"Fine," she told the poor woman. "Give Mr. Fleming this message for me. Tell him I said to eat dirt and die. Not very original, but the best I can do on the spur of the moment. I will not be at lunch tomorrow, as I have another appointment. If he wants this firm to work with him, he'll have to set up another time to meet."

There was a startled pause. "You want me to give him this message . . . now?"

"Please."

While Sherry waited, she finished off the bag of candy. This had suddenly become a war of wills, and she fully planned to win it, or lose the account trying. Not very professional, she decided, but then, Kit hadn't shown much professionalism himself when he'd used her to save his butt.

She was on hold a good five minutes, humming along to a Muzak version of "New York, New York." Just as she decided to hang up, the music cut off and Kit Fleming's voice resonated along the line. He was not in a good mood.

"I ought to fire you."

"You can't fire me, I don't work for you," she reminded him in a pleasant, even tone. "If you want to pull the account from this firm, that's your choice, Mr. Fleming. But let me just tell you this," she added, in a real friendly tone. "I will not be browbeaten, and I will not be yanked around at your whim.

Maybe for you the world begins and ends with Bella Luna, but it doesn't for me. When you learn to understand that, and *if* you still want me working on your account, then maybe we can come to terms. Until then, buzz off, bucko."

With that she hung up.

On the other end of the line, Kit pulled the phone from his ear and stared at it. Never, *never* had anyone stood up to him like this. He absolutely hated that he couldn't control this woman. That she had no fear of him. That she could take his business or leave it. That she could take him or leave him. That he wanted to take her with an intensity that both scared and excited him.

Slowly he returned the phone receiver to its cradle. He couldn't let her get away with this. Unfortunately, he didn't have much choice. Well, he could always yank the account. But that option held no appeal whatsoever, because he'd lose, too. Before he'd met her, Kit had only been vaguely aware of her reputation. Since dinner the other night, he'd made inquiries. Sherry Spencer was an advertising marvel. She'd won every major award her industry had to offer, and some they didn't.

She was basically a young genius. And she'd just told him to buzz off.

Thoroughly ticked, Kit dialed Simpson & Bailey, and swallowed the bitter bile of battered pride. When he heard Sherry's voice, he gruffly got right to the point. "How about dinner tomorrow night?"

It took her a few seconds to answer him, and the longer the time stretched, the more embarrassed he became. "Not another dinner party at Rachel's?"

"No."

"Now, no offense, Kit, but we don't get much work done at dinner."

"We will tomorrow night. I promise."

Again she hesitated. "Fine. Where and when?"

He wasn't prepared for those questions, because he hadn't expected to ask her to dinner again. "I'll have my secretary let you know," he answered, grabbing back at least a shred of control.

"Fine," she said. "Have your secretary leave the details with our receptionist."

And once again, she hung up.

Kit snarled. Then, to his utter amazement, he laughed. And it felt good.

Five

He'd brought Tiffany to dinner.

Sherry almost turned on her heel and marched out when she entered the swanky Moroccan restaurant in McLean, and spied Kit and the famous Tiffany with their heads close together, talking. Something stabbed through her, but she was intelligent enough to know she didn't want to identify it. She stiffened her spine, took a deep breath, and pointed out Kit's table to the hovering maître d'.

When Kit finally spotted her, he shot her a warning look before standing and putting a welcoming smile on his face that was as fake as Tiffany's breasts. He made the introductions, and Tiffany offered a limpwristed hand and a less than lukewarm smile. The woman was beautiful. Perfectly beautiful. She had honey-blond hair and huge green eyes that looked out from a face God had personally constructed.

Sherry returned the smile and accepted Kit's offer of a chair, all the while deciding which method of murder she'd find most satisfying. A lingering death definitely loomed in Kit Fleming's future.

"So, you're the advertising genius," Tiffany said, and her tone implied she considered the occupation one step below cleaning out sump pumps.

"That's me," Sherry answered the model, wondering what Kit was up to. Had he invited Tiffany because he considered it a foregone conclusion that she'd be signed as Bella Luna's next spokesmodel? Or had he brought her so that Sherry would have no chance to argue against spending a huge hunk of their advertising budget on an overpriced celebrity?

An exotic-looking waitress dressed in a harem outfit stopped to get her drink order. Kit's drink looked like a martini, and Tiffany had ordered white wine. Sherry sided with Kit on this one. She ordered a martini.

Beside the perfect Tiffany, she felt downright dowdy. She'd dressed too carefully again tonight, wearing her favorite Donna Karan blue silk. Tiffany wore a jumpsuit in emerald green that complemented her long hair and matched her eyes to perfection.

Kit wore his usual Armani power attire with an ease and grace that at the moment tore at her nerves. At the moment, good-looking men in general tore at her nerves. As did spokesmodels who gazed at good-looking men like they'd like to devour them. Oh, yes, Tiffany wanted Kit. And Sherry had the feeling that Tiffany usually got what Tiffany wanted.

There was no way Kit could misinterpret Tiffany's desire. She leaned toward him and smiled at him in that you-and-I-are-destined-for-the-bedroom way that only extremely confident women had. The strange thing was, Kit seemed to be ignoring the smoldering looks Tiffany shot him. His expression was polite, even a little distant. And when he turned his gaze on Sherry, she was shocked to see a passionate gleam in his beautiful eyes. Oh, Lord. He was *not* going to use her again as a buffer. No way. Kit Fleming could darn well take care of himself.

"Tiffany and I were just discussing concept," Kit said. "She likes the idea of combining a sexy campaign with some humorous undertones."

"Does she now?" Sherry said, trying very hard not to sound catty. Her drink arrived and she took a fortifying sip. She supposed she should feel at least somewhat happy that Kit had heard her the other day when she'd pitched the concept of using humor, but now that Tiffany agreed, the idea had lost some appeal.

"Good," she added, her eyes watering slightly from the healthy sip of martini she'd just downed. "What do you think about looking less than your best?"

Tiffany looked appalled. "What do you mean?"

"Here's how I see it," Sherry said, pulling a notepad out of her briefcase. "The model we choose will begin the first commercial looking less than stellar. No makeup, hair in a ponytail, etc. After using various Bella Luna health and beauty aids, we'll show how each product improves her appearance."

Tiffany stared at the rough sketches Sherry'd drawn. "Well—"

Sherry flipped a page. "I see a progression of commercials, as the model prepares to go out on a date. Interspersed in the commercials, we'll show the male model also preparing to pick her up. Buying flowers, wine, candy, tickets to a hit play, that sort of thing."

She flipped another page. "We build anticipation, until the audience can't wait to see these two people get together. When he finally shows up, the finale to the series of commercials, he's dazzled by this woman. She looks fantastic, she smells fantastic, her skin feels fantastic. And so on."

She glanced at Kit, who was also staring at her sketchpad. Finally he lifted his eyes to hers. "I love it."

Why that gave her so much pleasure, Sherry couldn't say. She was used to her ideas being adored by clients. And she always felt gratified. But right now, a sensation of delight rushed through her, and she had the feeling it had nothing to do with pride in her work, and everything to do with winning Kit's approval.

"Good," she said again. She returned her attention to Tiffany. "So, this series, if we go with it, will require the model to look less than her best at the beginning. We're not going to intentionally make her look awful, we're just going to show the audience the 'before Bella Luna' product."

Tiffany hated the idea. It showed like a neon sign in the pout she bestowed on Kit. "I'm not sure about this."

Kit smiled at her indulgently. "You couldn't look bad if you tried. All you'd be doing is going from beautiful to spectacular."

Tiffany preened. Sherry bristled. Tiffany bent into Kit. "For you, I'll do anything." Sherry leaned forward and somehow knocked Tiffany's water into her lap. "Oh, dear, I'm sorry," she said.

Tiffany jumped to her feet, with a horrified squeal. She

grabbed her napkin and dabbed at the water stains. "You clumsy—"

"The rest room's back there," Sherry interrupted, hiking her thumb.

Two bright red spots bloomed on Tiffany's perfect cheeks, and with a mumbled, "Excuse me," and a final glare, she hurried away.

Kit, whose mouth was slightly open, watched her go, then turned back to Sherry. "You did that on purpose."

"Darn right I did." She leaned toward him, ran a fingernail up his arm and batted her lashes at him. "For you, I'll do anything," she cooed. Then she sat back and glared at him. "What do you mean, bringing her to this meeting? Who cares how Tiffany feels about the campaign? And when did you make her an offer? Do you realize with the money we'd save on a lesser known model, we could buy more print space, even probably produce one additional commercial?"

"Tiffany's a name."

"Tiffany's a face and a body. One that appeals to men. Women will not identify with her, and will only resent you for using her to hype your products."

"So you say."

"So I know."

Sitting forward, Kit patted her hand in what she interpreted as a patronizing gesture. "Listen, I love your concept. Really. It's a fantastic idea. But I'm afraid I'm going to have to be adamant about this. I want a name."

"Or is it that you just want Tiffany?"

"Tiffany?" he said, his face blank. "Yes, right. I want Tiffany."

"That's convenient because Tiffany wants you, too." Could she get any more cheeky? And what did she care if the man and his model got it on?

Understanding finally dawned on his face. For a sophisticated man, he appeared rather dense at times. How could he not have picked up on Tiffany's signals? "You're wrong," he said. "Aren't you?"

Sherry laughed at him. "God, men are dumb."

His eyes clouded with irritation, and she had a hunch she'd just crossed the line. But then he mumbled, "Oh, Lord, I don't need this."

A little too pleased that he seemed truly unhappy, she sipped her drink and waited gleefully for Tiffany to return, thrilled to be able to witness his discomfort.

He looked around the restaurant, and when he saw Tiffany making her way back to the table, he slid his chair closer to Sherry.

"Hey!" she complained. "What do you think you're doing?"

He looked at her, his eyes pleading. "Just once more, okay?"

"No way," she said, wondering why her pulse jumped. "I'm not bailing you out again. Learn to fight your own battles, Casanova."

"Please, Sherry," he cajoled. "I don't want to deal with this, right now."

"Tough. If you want a shield, buy one."

"You look fantastic tonight," he said, before leaning over and kissing her.

The jerk! The condescending jerk! The condescending, wonderful smelling jerk! She would have liked to bite his lip, but she found herself enjoying his mouth on hers. The man had a lot of personality flaws, but he sure knew how to kiss.

The clearing of a throat brought them apart. If looks could kill, Sherry'd be keeling over right about then.

Kit laughed, a little self-deprecatingly. "Sorry about that. Sometimes I tend to forget myself with Sherry. She hates that I can't separate business and pleasure, but can you blame me?"

Sherry kicked him under the table. He grunted slightly, but otherwise kept his loving smile plastered in place. He stood and helped Tiffany into her seat. Sherry stood and started stuffing her briefcase.

Kit looked at her with evident alarm. "What are you doing?"

"Leaving."

"You can't!"

She smiled up at him, cupping his cheek. "Sweetheart, I have so much work to do. Since you like this campaign, I'll just leave you and Tiffany to hammer out the details. You understand, don't you?"

"Sure," he said, but his eyes promised revenge. "If you have to go."

"I do."

"See you later, pumpkin," he said, then kissed Sherry one final time. "I'll be home after I take Tiffany back to her hotel."

Sherry nearly sputtered her outrage. Now he was pretending to live with her! She clutched his lapel and drew him down to her. "You are a dead man," she whispered through her fake smile.

"I look forward to it, too, sugar. Have a bottle of wine breathing."

"That wine will be the only thing breathing if you drop on by."

"Wait up for me, lollipop."

Dead. The man was as good as dead, and it would be justifiable homicide to Sherry's way of thinking. Her cheeks ached from the fake smile. She waggled her fingers at Tiffany, who looked like she wanted to breathe fire. "Nice meeting you, Tiff."

And with that she got out of there before she killed Kit Fleming in front of witnesses.

> Jud lifted Lorna into his arms. "Never leave me again, Lorna. Without you I'm nothing. Marry me, my heart. Make me the luckiest man alive."
>
> "Yes, oh, yes. I'll marry you. Oh, Jud, I love you so much."
>
> "You'll have years and years to prove that to me."
>
> "Starting now."
>
> "Starting now," Jud agreed, as he carried her across the meadow toward home.
>
> THE END

Sherry sighed contentedly, then put the book down on the coffee table. Nothing soothed her agitated nerves better than a good romance novel. Someday, she'd have a hot romance all her own. And she prayed it would be as satisfying as the books she read, with the promise of happily ever after.

A girl could dream, couldn't she?

The phone rang, and still in a sensual sort of lethargy, she picked up her cordless. "Hello?"

"I'm out front," Kit Fleming said, effectively popping her dreamy bubble. "Can we talk?"

"When hell forms icebergs," she replied, her agitation returning in full force.

"I can explain."

"What's to explain? You're too much of a coward to do your own dirty work, and you hide behind me."

"Come on, Sherry."

She checked her watch. Two hours had passed since she'd returned home. Either they'd had a very long, very cozy dinner, or Kit had done just a bit more than drop Tiffany off at her hotel. "You get five minutes."

She supposed she was an idiot for letting him in, but the opportunity to tell the lug off was too precious to pass up. She looked down at her gym shorts and faded T-shirt and shrugged off the desire to run put something more flattering on. What did she care what he thought of her clothes?

A moment later he knocked, and the sound seemed to echo in her chest. She pulled open the door and glared at him. But then she saw the peace offering in his hand. Somehow he'd gotten his hands on a bottle of red wine, and he held it out with an optimistic smile.

In that instant, her heart melted. He looked so darn adorable with that hopeful expression on his face that she didn't have it in her to blister him the way he deserved. She took the wine from him. "Thank you," she said grudgingly, mad at herself for being such a sucker.

"May I come in?"

Sherry stepped back. Kit stepped forward. Once. Then

stopped in his tracks. It didn't take a genius to notice where his attention had strayed: straight to her legs. Which embarrassed her, because she didn't much care for her legs. They didn't travel all the way to her armpits, the way Tiffany's did. And the nickname Sean Robertson had given her in high school still made her mad. He'd dubbed her Pogo, because he'd said she had stick legs.

"Something wrong?" she asked Kit.

He blinked, then cleared his throat. "No, not at all," he said, his voice a bit hoarse. He entered her apartment, and she shut the door.

"Glass of wine?" she asked him, then turned just in time to find him looking over her rear end just as thoroughly. The man was a lech. A very cute lech, but a lech regardless.

"Yes, please," he said, not even trying to mask his appreciation. Or fake appreciation. He was probably just attempting to flatter her into not being angry at him. She had to keep in mind that this man was a consummate actor.

"Have a seat," she said, waving at her couch.

Sherry opened the wine in the kitchen, poured two goblets and brought them out to the living room. And caught Kit leafing through the romance novel she'd just finished reading.

Quickly she deposited the glasses on the table and grabbed the book from him, stuffing it under her couch cushion.

When he looked up at her, his eyes sparkled. "So, the tough little ad exec has a romantic heart."

She cocked her hip and her fists hit her waist. "Got a problem with that?"

He tilted his head a little in an assessing manner. "You really believe in all that romance stuff?"

"Of course, don't you?"

He snorted rudely. "Not a chance."

Sherry assessed him right back. "Then I feel sorry for you."

His jaw went slack. "Feel sorry for me? Lady, I'm not the one who's going to be sadly disappointed when I learn that happily ever after doesn't exist."

"It exists for my parents. They've been married thirty-eight years, and they're still devoted to each other."

"Then they're the exception," he retorted, starting to look uncomfortable. "All I know is, it will never exist for me."

Sherry bit her bottom lip, oddly piqued by his words. "I changed my mind. I don't feel sorry for you. I feel sorry for the women in your life."

He loosened his tie and slipped open his collar button. "Save your pity. The women I get involved with know the rules up front."

One brow arched, she said, "Oh, please. I'm dying of curiosity. What rules would those be?"

He raised his hand quickly, and started rattling off his rules as he ticked off his fingers. Sherry had a feeling he'd indeed preached these "rules" plenty of times. "One, no promises of monogamy. I'm not a one-woman man. Two, no promises of commitment. I have no desire to hang a noose around my neck. And three, no promises of love. Personally, I think the emotion is highly overrated."

Sherry burst out laughing, even as her heart started giving her a hard time. "What a crock."

Scowling, he said, "At least I'm honest about it."

She tossed him a look of pure pity, then shook her head. "Amazing," she murmured. Then she picked up her wine and sat down on the couch, tucking her legs under her. "So, what are you doing here, Mr. Footloose-and-Fancy-Free?"

He loosened his tie some more. "Just came to say thanks."

"What you should be saying is, 'I'm sorry.'"

"That, too. Listen, I really appreciate the heads-up, tonight. I'm not usually so blind."

She sipped her wine. It was delicious. "Most men would kill to have Tiffany come on to them."

"Which is exactly why I want to use her in the Christmas ad blitz."

Shaking her head, she said, "You just don't get it, do you? You're not trying to fulfill men's fantasies. You're trying to fulfill women's. If you'd stop thinking with your zipper for one minute, you'd see that she's all wrong for the market."

He choked on his wine. "Thi-thinking with my zipper!"

She patted his back. "Thinking like a man. You've got to approach this from a woman's perspective."

Blinking his watery eyes, he said, "We're never going to agree on this."

"I could convince you."

He looked at her suspiciously. "How?"

"Let's do a test run. Nothing fancy, just sort of a walk-through. We'll shoot two ads, one with Tiffany, one with another model. Then we conduct a focus group made up of your target customers. Let them decide."

"That'll cost money."

"Not as much as hiring Tiffany for all the ads, and having them bomb."

He considered that for a moment. "All right, you're on."

"Yes!" she cried. She tapped his temple. "I knew there was a brain hidden deep down in there somewhere!"

Kit glowered at the infuriating woman again, and set down his glass. Grabbing her shoulders, he turned her to face him. Her breasts jiggled a little under her T-shirt. She wasn't wearing a bra.

Kit's mouth went dry. He had to take a moment to remember what he'd meant to say to her. "Are you calling me dumb?" he asked.

Her eyes glittered devilishly. "No. Just a man."

Oh, he felt like a man all right. A man holding a beautiful woman who *wasn't wearing a bra.* Hormones danced like popping corn through his body.

Damn. Why did this lady affect him so much? Every time he got near her, his body started heating up and his thoughts turned purely sensual. She made something in his chest soften, and something else somewhat lower go rock hard.

Why? She wasn't even close to being as beautiful as Tiffany, but Tiffany hadn't done a thing for him. In fact, when Tiffany had made the ultimate pass at her hotel tonight—obviously not concerned about the morality of stealing another woman's man—he'd actually been filled with a quiet distaste.

For some reason, Sherry appealed to him like no woman

he'd known. It was more than just her intelligence, more than her physical beauty. An elusive quality she possessed called to him, made him want to learn everything he could about her. Like the noises she made when she was mindlessly aroused.

Suddenly he realized they were staring at each other wordlessly. He couldn't have that. If they weren't going to talk, they'd have to entertain themselves some other way. He pulled her to him and kissed her. Instantly he was lost in the lush softness of her mouth. His fingers gently stroked her cheeks as he slanted her head and traced her lips with his tongue.

Throbbing excitement pounded through him. He grasped her thigh and pulled her leg over his lap so she straddled him. His hands moved to her hips, and he rocked their lower bodies together, until they both gasped.

Her arms wound around his neck and she pressed into him. Even through his suit coat, he could feel her unbound breasts crush against his chest.

"Sherry, Sherry," he whispered lifting his hips to press into that soft place that was all woman. An explosion of sensation erupted inside him. He was rapidly losing control.

Control. Something close to panic swelled in his chest. He couldn't lose control. Without it, he had nothing. Without it, he was vulnerable. And Kit never planned to put himself in a vulnerable position again as long as he lived. Vulnerability made a person weak.

With iron will, he wrestled for control over his body, over everything this woman made him feel. It was a more difficult task than he'd have thought possible, but he finally conquered his need. He pushed her hips away from his and broke the kiss. Her eyes fluttered open, almost black with passion.

He had to get away from her. He couldn't sit here looking at her, knowing what it felt like to be kissing her intimately. Sherry Spencer was a dangerous woman. She made him want things he'd never wanted before, made him want to trust in the honest desire in her eyes, made him want to just let go.

"Kit?" she said, her voice husky and puzzled at once. "What's wrong?"

He knew his eyes were probably wild with horror. God, he'd almost lost it with her. He lifted her off of him and set her on the couch. Practically jumping to his feet, he glanced at his watch. "I—I forgot, there's somewhere I have to be. I'm sorry, you go ahead and . . . enjoy the wine. I, uh, I'll be in touch."

With that, he fled her apartment.

Sherry stared after Kit, bewildered, bemused and achingly unfulfilled. What had just happened here? First he kissed her, with no prodding on her part. But it had felt so utterly wonderful, she couldn't bring herself to object. And then the kiss turned deeply intimate, this time with help from her. She'd filled so fast with yearning, she'd wanted him desperately.

And then, he'd stopped. Just like that. Bang. Over.

What the heck was going on? Kit had looked suddenly terrified, but she couldn't imagine why. It wasn't the terror of a coward, but the terror of a man facing his worst fear. How had she gone from being the woman in his arms—on his lap and loving it, for criminy's sake—to being his worst nightmare? Color flooded her face as she suddenly realized how she had behaved. She'd never abandoned herself so completely with a man before. Especially a man she wasn't certain she liked in the least.

Well, he'd obviously helped prove one thing. Sherry Spencer was capable of loveless lust. Put a pair of enigmatic eyes and sexy lips in front of her, and who knew how far from grace she'd fall? Well, she wouldn't fall again. She was done experimenting with the wanton side of her nature. Kit Fleming could just find some other hussy to toy with. She wasn't playing any longer.

As she picked up her wine she tried not to feel so darn disappointed.

Six

Tiffany was what a generous spirit might call a sensitive actress. Not feeling too generous, Sherry chose to characterize her as a royal pain in the butt. The model couldn't act at all, she wouldn't appear in front of the camera sans makeup, and she was still trying her level best to start something with the CEO of Bella Luna.

Not only that, but Tiffany seemed to hold Sherry personally responsible for the fact that Tiffany basically had to audition for the part. Sherry didn't mind, merely because she *was* personally responsible. She did not want Tiffany doing the ads. Honesty forced her to admit that her wish was not entirely professional, but the decision was.

If the jerk across the studio being fawned over by yet another female—this time the hairstylist—chose Tiffany over the *real* actress, Sherry would have her proof that he had the brains of a blade of grass.

Three weeks had passed since that disastrous encounter in her apartment, and in that time Kit had taken to avoiding her with a zealousness that aggravated her to high heaven.

He'd suddenly decided that conference calls were a perfectly acceptable way to hold meetings, and he hadn't coerced her to go out to dinner once since then. She'd put together this dry run in record time, and all she'd gotten for her trouble was a gruff, "It's about time."

She'd scoured talent agencies looking for the perfect actress for Ms. Bella Luna, and Kit had taken one look at the woman's photo—sent to him by messenger—and called to say, "I wanted a blonde."

In other words, he was being a total, unmitigated jerk.

What bothered Sherry most was she had no idea what she'd

done to deserve this treatment. She wanted to avoid him at all costs, too, but only if she got to be the one doing the avoiding. Instead, it was a constant battle to get him to take her calls, and she took it as a personal insult that he dreaded the thought of sharing the same space with her.

Which made his appearance here at the studio today rather surprising.

The director stopped the actress and the cameras several times before they finally managed a complete run-through. But Sherry felt the final product would be good. The actress had just the right level of excitement over her date, and nervousness that she'd make a good impression. She ended the scene beside a clawfoot tub filling with steaming water. Gazing at the bottle of Satin Sleek bubble bath in her hand, she smiled and delivered her final line. "Come on, baby, make my date." Then she dropped the towel, and stepped into the tub.

"Cut!"

"What do you think?" Kit asked from behind her.

Sherry jumped, then turned, her heart in her throat. She looked up into hazel eyes and felt lost. Her lips parted, but she couldn't seem to get words past them. Probably because her brain had ceased functioning. She was aware only of sensation. Of the heat of his body, so close after all this time. Of his scent, clean and male and provocative. Of the buzzing in her ears, as she stared up into his handsome face. Of the staccato beat of her heart.

"What?" she finally asked in a croak.

He didn't answer right away, just seemed to search her face for she didn't know what. "I asked . . . uh, what you . . . thought."

"About what?"

"I don't know."

They stared at each other, and for Sherry, the rest of the world vanished. Nothing existed but them and the thrumming tension that coiled around them.

Something strong and sexual existed between them, and suddenly Sherry understood Kit's fear. He was afraid of this.

Why, she didn't know. All she knew was that the chemistry between them spooked him.

All of the anger that had built toward him the last few weeks slipped quietly out of her. "You're afraid of me," she whispered, a little awed by her insight.

"Damn right I am," he murmured in response.

"Why?"

He swallowed. "I want you too damn much."

The tightness in her chest eased. No one had ever wanted her too much. A sense of rightness almost overwhelmed her. "Is that a bad thing?" she asked.

"Very bad."

"Why?"

"I don't like the feeling."

Huh? He didn't like feeling attracted to her? Why not? What was wrong with a little physical desire? Did she scare him because he was used to being attracted to more beautiful women? Did he not like desiring intimacy with an average woman? Should she be utterly insulted or flattered? She decided now wasn't the time to ask, as it was now Tiffany's turn.

"She's still wearing too much makeup," Sherry called to the director.

He turned, a rueful grin on his face. "You try to wipe it off her."

Several minutes later, Sherry had to suppress a victorious "Yes!" as she watched Tiffany botch her lines again and again. Her movements were stiff, her smile false, her delight forced. She stunk.

Sherry glanced up at Kit to see if he wanted to go ahead and just fire Tiffany now, and was horrified to find him grinning as if he were pleased with the model's performance. She couldn't decide if he was happy. Tiffany was so bad, or if he thought Tiffany was next year's Oscar winner. When he glanced down and shot Sherry a smug smile, Sherry almost choked. He really thought the woman had talent!

Stifling rising panic, Sherry glanced around at the other men in the studio. All of them were gazing raptly at Tiffany, entranced. Good God, how stupid could men be? This was not good.

When they finally wrapped Tiffany's segment of the commercial, the applause from the male members of the crew nearly brought down the roof. Sherry glanced around, jaw slack. She locked gazes with the only other sane person in the studio, the actress. She looked at Sherry as if the world had lost its collective mind, which to Sherry's way of thinking, it had. At least the male half of it had. She rolled her eyes and nodded encouragingly at the young woman, who smiled, looking a little less upset.

While the crew got busy, changing sets for the male actor's takes, Kit turned to Sherry again, triumph gleaming in his eyes. "Well, what do you have to say about that?" he asked. His tone was so condescending and smug, she wanted to belt him one.

"I say, if I ever needed proof that men's thinking takes place below the belt, I've just been handed it," she retorted, before turning and stalking away.

Sherry, Kit, and the director of the research facility they'd hired to run the focus group were all seated in stuffed swivel chairs at a long conference table, filled with platters of food and jugs of water and fruit juice. Directly in front of them was a one-way mirror, allowing them to watch the group seated around a circular table in the next room.

The participants were also being fed. There were fifteen women—besides the moderator of the session—all ranging in ages from twenty-five to thirty-nine, and broken down into ethnic groups closely approximating the national population.

The focus group had just begun, and the moderator was explaining how they would proceed and what was expected of the recruits. She wanted them to watch two commercials, then fill out the questionnaire before them, and then an impromptu discussion would take place.

At least to the participants, the discussion would seem impromptu. They didn't know that the moderator was highly trained at eliciting answers to questions Sherry and Jim Forbes had formulated.

"Why couldn't Jim come again?" Sherry asked Kit, seated beside her.

"Lamaze class with his wife," Kit answered absently, popping a cube of cheddar cheese in his mouth, followed quickly by a plump red grape.

She eyed his attire. This was the first time she'd seen Kit dressed in anything other than a suit, and she had to grudgingly admit that he looked just as delicious in casual clothes. Even if she was slightly insulted that he had so little respect for this process, and didn't believe that business attire was necessary.

He wore gray pleated chinos and a wine-colored chambray shirt, sleeves rolled to reveal a very expensive-looking Cartier wristwatch. His forearms were powerful and masculine, with a light sprinkling of chestnut hair. His fingernails were well-groomed, but didn't appear professionally manicured. Somehow she liked the image of him caring for his own nails. Why, she hadn't a clue.

Sherry herself had felt the need to keep this all very professional, so she had worn her cream tailored suit, with a peach silk blouse underneath. She'd chosen this outfit on purpose. Her cream pumps sported the highest heels, and Sherry had felt the need for height. She was tired of having to drop her head back so far to look at Kit when they were standing.

Kit used his height as a weapon. She'd learned that early on. He liked towering over her and trying to intimidate her. She found that fact very irritating, if futile. In her opinion, the bigger they were, the harder they fell.

Still, she was nervous tonight. It had been two weeks since the preliminary shoot, and in that time she'd grown more and more worried over Kit's constant insistence that Tiffany had proved she could act. Even when they'd viewed the edited videos this afternoon, Kit and Jim had both appeared pleased with her performance. *Men.*

Sherry prayed the research company had recruited straight-thinking women.

The meeting got under way. The participants watched the ads in silence. Sherry tried to gauge their reactions, but they were expressionless, which made her palms sweat. She reached into her briefcase and pulled out a Mounds bar.

Kit glanced at her, his brows raised as he watched her bite into the chocolate. She understood his consternation. There was enough food in front of them to feed a regiment. But there wasn't an ounce of chocolate among it.

She savored the taste, letting it soothe her frayed nerves. One of these days her metabolism was going to start protesting her chocolate addiction, and she'd have to find a less fattening substitute. She didn't look forward to it.

The moderator turned up the lights and instructed the participants to fill out their questionnaires. The longest ten minutes of Sherry's life ensued.

Finally, all the women's pencils were down and the moderator began the discussion. "Well, what did you think of the two ads?"

One by one, the women gave their general impressions. They liked the concept, liked the whimsical tone. That was good. They weren't dissing Tiffany. That was bad.

Kit sat forward, his face a study in stern concentration. Sherry sat back, and took out a bag of Reese's Pieces.

"What do you think of the female model in the first version?"

"That's Tiffany," one lady answered.

"Right. Did all of you recognize her?"

A chorus of yeses and nodding heads followed.

Kit shot Sherry a triumphant smirk. Sherry gobbled more candy.

"And, what did you think about her performance?" the moderator asked. When no one spoke up, she added, "Anyone, jump in."

One tiny Asian woman timidly raised her hand. The moderator encouraged her with a nod. "She . . . can't act."

Kit made a strange gurgling sound and sat back. Sherry made a happy gurgling sound and sat forward.

The floodgates opened. "I don't believe for a minute she uses those products," one woman chimed in.

"Me either," said another, the youngest of the group. "No amount of makeup is going to make me look like Tiffany."

Kit dropped his pen in disgust. Sherry shook a victorious fist.

The director sitting beside Sherry excused herself, leaving the two of them alone in the room. Sherry put her bag of candy away, suddenly hungry for something other than chocolate. Biting into a beef hor d'oeuvre rolled with cream cheese and olives, she chewed slowly, before turning to face Kit. "What do you think?"

His face remained impassive, but his eyes gleamed with genuine puzzlement. "I don't think anything, yet."

Sherry nodded and went back to munching on the finger food, realizing she hadn't eaten anything but candy all day because she'd been too nervous about tonight. Suddenly, she was ravenous. Within minutes it became blessedly obvious that the women in the focus group could identify with the actress more than they could with Tiffany. As Sherry had predicted, they resented the unfair comparison, and one even went so far as to say, "To me, the commercial with Tiffany in it is a lie."

"Uncle," Kit muttered.

Sherry wanted, *needed,* to gloat. But Kit's concession gave her enough satisfaction without embarrassing him further. "Pardon me?"

"You win," Kit said.

Sherry decided graciousness was in order. "At least they liked the concept."

"Yeah, at least they liked that."

Suddenly, she felt a warmth at her nape, and realized Kit had laid his palm there beneath her bun. She turned to him, eyes wide. "What are you doing?"

"What I've been dreaming about doing," he murmured, "for a long time."

"Kit, wait."

He ignored her, even as his hand massaged her neck, and

his other came up to cup her face. "Do you know, I haven't had a good night's sleep since the day I met you?" he said in a growly voice that vibrated in her ear.

"But—"

"You make me crazy," he continued. "I think about you all day, I dream about you at night."

"The focus group—"

"Is being videotaped," he interrupted, his thumb sweeping down her cheek.

Sherry's eyes shut, as she tried to block the sight of him looking down at her with sudden passion. "Kit," she whispered, "don't do this."

His thumb rubbed across her lower lip. "So beautiful. So tempting." He blew out a ragged breath. "You make me crazy."

"I . . . thought you hated that about me."

"I love that about you. I hate it about me."

He pulled her to her feet, then replaced his stroking thumb with his lips, his tongue. Sherry gasped low in her throat as desire coursed through her. Deep, earth-shaking desire. Before she could control herself, she wound her arms around his neck and answered his passionate kiss.

But a sudden—not to mention rather unwelcome—burst of sanity blew through her, and Sherry pushed him away.

"Sherry?"

She turned her back on him. "Just . . . leave me alone for a minute. I need to think here."

If she'd expected him to protest, she was sadly mistaken. He didn't say a word. So she hugged herself and thought things through.

Why would Kit want to come on to her? She knew it wasn't overwhelming attraction, not when he could have his pick of women at the crook of a finger. She replayed each private kiss in her mind, trying to discover a pattern to his seduction. What was he up to? What was his game? What did he want from her?

Most importantly, what did she want from him? Considering the way he tried to control her—

Sherry's jaw dropped open, as the fog vanished from her

head. Of course! Again she revisited each and every time he'd kissed her when they hadn't had an audience, and found the one common denominator. Every time had been immediately after a situation where he perceived he'd lost a measure of control.

Sherry smacked the table, then whirled to face him.

"What?" he said, a deep vee between his eyebrows.

"By gum, that's it!"

"What's it?"

She allowed herself a smug smile. "I've finally got your number."

He seemed to go stiff, a tic starting in his jaw. Then she could tell he was visibly trying to make himself relax. He drummed his thumbs on the table in a vain attempt to appear unconcerned. "Is that right?" he drawled.

"That's right, Mr. Fleming, I've got you pegged."

"Why don't you tell me what you think you know about me?"

Sherry pointed at him. "You, sir, are a control freak."

He went stiff again, his thumbs giving up their drumming. "You think so?"

"I know it, pal."

"What gives you that idea?"

Sherry clucked. "Isn't it obvious? Every time you feel like you're not in control of a situation, you try to seduce me. Because you know—" She folded her arms over her chest.

"Because I know . . . what?" he asked, a grin playing at his lips. If he wasn't careful, before he knew it he'd be smiling, and then his face would likely crack.

"Never mind. Just admit I'm right." She thrust out her chin, because even though she was happy to have figured him out, the knowledge that he had ulterior motives for wanting to get close to her hurt just a little. "Just admit that if you could manipulate and control me in the board room, you'd have no desire to try to get me in a bedroom."

His gaze swept over her features as he leaned a lean hip against the table. "That's where you're wrong, sweetheart. I'd want you no matter what."

Her heart started thudding almost painfully. "I don't believe you."

He shook his head. "If you want to accuse me of anything, try tenacity."

Sherry frowned. "Tenacity? What do you mean?"

He shoved off from the table and walked to the door. The click of the lock reverberated through the room. He turned back and began stalking her. "You know, tenacity. The relentless pursuit of a goal or goals."

She shouldn't ask. She knew it with every fiber in her. But her lips and her brain didn't seem to be on speaking terms at the moment. "And just what is this goal you plan to pursue relentlessly?"

His eyes glittered. "To make you scream with pleasure when you come."

Seven

Sherry very seldom found herself at a loss for words. But right now she was completely flummoxed. She couldn't have heard him correctly. "Excuse me?"

"You heard me," he said, crossing his arms and smirking at her.

"You . . . are . . . the . . . most . . . conceited—"

He held up his hands, palms out. "What's so conceited about wanting to give a woman pleasure?"

"This isn't about giving pleasure, buster. It's about control."

One of his brows lifted. "Wanting to make you fall apart in my arms means I need to be in control?"

"Absolutely." She tsked, shaking her head. "Let me ask you this. If we ever got together . . . that way, would you let me tie you up? Handcuff you?"

That stopped him in his predatory tracks. His eyes gleamed with a hilarious mixture of humor and horror. He tugged at his collar. "Uh, yeah, sure, if you're into that. You're not, are you?"

"Oh, yeah," she said, taking a step toward him, while he took a giant step backward, nearly knocking over a chair.

Two could play at this control thing. If he thought he could manipulate her with just a smoldering look and a deep, wet kiss, he could just think again.

Sherry wasn't into teaching lessons as a rule. But this big lug needed to be taught a thing or two. One, that she could play seductress, and maintain control of the situation. Two, that she could kiss him six ways from Sunday, and still remain unaffected.

He definitely needed to be taught that he couldn't control her. Not in a board room, not in a bedroom, and certainly not in a focus group room, where they were *supposed* to be watching a discussion on health and beauty products.

"Kit," she whispered, backing him right to the wall. "Kiss me."

Kit's body went taut. He groaned and yanked her to him, his features set in a pained expression. He stared into her eyes for one heart-stopping moment, before settling his mouth over hers.

Sherry told herself to maintain control. She told herself not to feel, just act. She told herself that she could handle his ravishing lips, his seeking tongue.

As her arms twined around his neck, she told herself to shut up.

Kit's arm banded around her, lifting her to her tiptoes. Then he swung her around so her back was to the table. Sherry felt his arm sweep behind her, and then she barely registered a crash of sorts. Before she could determine the source of the noise, he grasped her waist and set her on the table.

His hands gripped her knees and spread her thighs apart and he moved between her legs. Breaking the kiss, he gazed down at her, and she gasped at the fiery fever in his eyes. He looked like a man possessed.

He grabbed the lapels of her jacket and shoved it off her shoulders, trapping her hands at her sides. His eyes burned her wherever they roamed, his hands branded her wherever they touched.

He was all primal male, and Sherry responded to him like the wanton female she'd so recently discovered she could be. Her skirt bunched at her hips, her breasts thrust out as her back remained arched in this imprisoned state.

"Kit . . ." she breathed, her head falling back.

His hand cupped her breast as his lips worked down her chin to her throat. He breathed words she couldn't comprehend against her skin, but she understood the sentiment. They were out of control. Both of them.

His mouth closed over the silk covering her bra, and she gasped again as his tongue teased her nipple until it tightened and ached. Lightning bolts of desire arced from her chest to her core, streaking in almost painful paths through her.

With her hands trapped she was helpless to push him away . . . or hold him closer. A swelling and throbbing began between her legs that wanted only to be released. She desperately needed him to touch her there, but she was too crazy to form the words.

As if he read her fevered mind, his hand slid up her thigh, under her skirt, to cup her very center. "Oh!" Sherry cried. "Oh, Kit!"

He released her breast and covered her mouth with his own. Sherry vaguely realized that he was probably trying to keep her from being heard throughout the building.

Smart move on his part, because she desperately wanted to scream.

He continued to massage her through her pantyhose, one finger, up and down, making her want him with a ferocity that engulfed her.

It suddenly occurred to Sherry that every move he made was controlled and calculated to bring her all the pleasure. Though she had no doubt he was aroused, he wasn't nearly as out of his mind as she was.

Her plan had backfired. And she didn't care.

And she didn't want to take this ride on her own. She wrapped her legs around his hips and dragged him against her, and they both gasped as his steel-hard arousal jutted against her ultra-sensitive center.

"Christ," he hissed, gazing down on her with wild eyes. "It's too good."

"It's just right," she rasped out.

"Sherry—"

"Tiffany's merely a sex kitten," Sherry heard a woman say through the speaker. Reality crashed in on her as she realized what they were doing. They were coming close to making love on a table, with only a glass barrier between them and a group of women.

All of her passion and desire vanished, replaced by utter mortification. Kit must not have registered her suddenly stiff body, because he was still grasping her hips and rocking into her, muttering harsh sex words into her neck.

"Stop!" Sherry cried, kicking him in the rear with the heel of her pump.

Kit straightened and stared at her as if he didn't recognize her. As if she'd lost her mind. Perhaps she had.

"We have company," she whispered, trying desperately to get her jacket back up to her shoulders, and to cover the wet circle overtop her left breast.

Kit glanced toward the door, then back at Sherry, his desire replaced by irritation. "What company?"

"Behind us, you idiot!"

He looked up. "So what? They can't see or hear us."

"That's not the point!" She finally succeeded in straightening her jacket, then pushed him back and hopped off the table, tugging her skirt lower. "I can't believe this." She glared self-righteously and pointed at him. "It won't work. So don't try it again."

With that she snapped shut her briefcase and yanked it off the table. "I've heard enough. If you still decide to use Tiffany as your spokesmodel, you're on your own. I've done all I can do to convince you it's a mistake."

"Sherry, wait," he said, following right behind her as she marched to the door and started fumbling with the lock.

"Leave me alone!" she demanded, finally winning the war with the deadbolt. Striding down the hall toward the front door, she ignored Kit's attempts to stop her. She had to get away from this place, this man.

The director of the facility emerged from a room carrying a coffee mug and stopped as she saw the two of them leaving. "Sherry?"

Grinding to a halt, Sherry managed a polite smile on her face. "Sorry, Gail, I have to go. You did a fantastic job, as usual. I'll look forward to getting the video and the tabulated results of the questionnaires tomorrow."

She checked her watch. "Oops, I'm late! How about if you escort Mr. Fleming back to the observation room?" She fluttered her fingers. "Toodles." Before either of them could respond, she sailed right by a gaping Gail and hightailed it to the front door and freedom.

The parking lot seemed darker than usual tonight, full of ominous shadows. Sherry swallowed a sudden wave of apprehension as she crossed to her car, digging into her briefcase for a much needed candy bar.

She didn't see the pothole in front of her. Not until the heel of her shoe landed in it and stuck. Off balance, she dropped her briefcase, let out a squawk, and promptly fell forward.

Pain shot up her right leg from her ankle and she cried out again. Gravel embedded itself in her palms and her knees, but she barely noticed. Not when her ankle was throbbing in agonizing bursts.

She whimpered as she tried to push to her feet. She failed, and instead twisted and landed ignominiously on her rump.

"Sherry, my God, are you all right?"

Oh, great. Just great. She couldn't even humiliate herself privately. "I'm fine," she said, then proved herself a liar by mewling when she tested her ankle.

"You are not fine," Kit said, hunkering down beside her. "Come on, let's get you to a hospital."

"No!" she nearly shouted. Taking a deep breath she lowered her voice. "Please, if you'd just help me to my car."

The concern etched on his face was rather endearing. "Just sit still a moment and let me check. What'd you hurt?"

She pointed at her ankle. "I think I just twisted it a little." She brushed gravel from her knees, noting that her stockings were ruined. "Help me up, please, Kit"

He helped her up all right. Straight into his arms.

She wiggled. "Put me down!"

"No," he said, bending to grab her briefcase.

If her ankle didn't hurt so much, she might have enjoyed being held in his strong embrace, might have appreciated the heat from his body and the wonderful scent of his aftershave. As it was, she let out another little whimper and rested her head on his chest. His heartbeat, strong and true, against her ear.

When she heard the sound of a car door opening, she raised her head and opened her eyes. "What are you doing?" she asked. "This is *your* car."

"I'm driving you to the emergency room."

"No way! Listen, it's already feeling better."

"Right," he said, stuffing her into the passenger seat.

She tried to scramble out of the car, but he blocked her with his body. "I'm taking you, sweetheart," he said. "You can't drive with a hurt ankle."

She hadn't thought of that. Unfortunately, Kit was right. She didn't think she could stand to depress the gas pedal. "Okay, fine," she conceded. "But take me home, not to a hospital, all right?"

He glared at her for a moment. "Fine. I'll take you home."

He sprinted around the front of the car, and Sherry marveled that at a time like this, she could still take a moment to appreciate the way the man moved. He was way too sexy for her peace of mind.

What was wrong with her? Why couldn't she control herself when it came to Kit? Why did she forget everything but the man himself when he touched her?

She felt so confused. She didn't understand the emotions inside her. She felt frightened. Not being able to control this growing attraction to Kit scared her to death. And she felt just a little piqued. Because he knew quite well how much he turned her on.

As they headed from Vienna to Falls Church, Kit seemed content to drive in silence, which was just as well. So many jumbled thoughts were bouncing through her head, she didn't know if she'd be able to hold up her end of the conversation.

Kit would bet a good bit of his fortune that very few things fazed Sherry Spencer. Right now, she looked as if she'd just been walloped with a two-by-four. And he didn't think it had a thing to do with her ankle.

"Sherry?" he finally said, as he watched her carefully. If her eyes got any bigger, they'd cover her whole face.

He pulled into the guest lot of her condo, and parked. Then

he reached out to touch her. She flinched, pressing herself against the passenger door. Obviously he'd frightened her, but he didn't know why. He'd expected outrage more than fright. He liked watching her outraged, and he knew right off that he did not like watching her frightened. "What's wrong?" he finally asked. "Your ankle?"

She shook her head. "No. Well, yes, but that's not it."

"Then what?"

"This . . . this whole night has been a disaster."

Well, that wasn't exactly an ego booster. Kit decided to intentionally misunderstand. "Why? You won. Tiffany's out."

"That's not what I mean, and you know it."

"I'm sorry," he said finally. "I was out of line tonight. But you have to admit, you participated."

It took a moment for Sherry to respond, but she finally managed it. She punched at her seat belt until it released her. Reaching for the door handle, she glared at him. "You pushed me to it."

He sighed, clamping his hand around her arm to keep her anchored in place. "Sherry, I'm a man. You're a beautiful woman. I can't help it that I'm attracted to you. At least I'm honest about it."

"You want to control me."

"I want to make love to you. If you equate that with control, that's your problem, not mine. I want sex, Sherry. Plain, old-fashioned, sweaty, mind-blowing sex. With you."

She stared at him, apparently turning his words over in her mind. "And exactly what would be the rules in this situation?"

Kit frowned. "The usual ones, of course."

"I see. You mean the ones about"—she lifted her hand, ticking them off on her fingers—"no monogamy, no commitment, no talk of . . . feelings besides lust."

"Right," he said, pleased she remembered.

She smiled. "I've got one more to add to your list."

Feeling magnanimous, he nodded. "Which is?"

"Take a hike," she said, turning up her nose. "I'm not playing by your rules, you egomaniacal . . . man! So you can just take a real long hike."

"Damn," he muttered. He'd blown it. Honesty really didn't work well with women. They preferred subterfuge. Why had he thought Sherry would be any different? Strangely disappointed that she was acting typically female, he decided to let it go, for now. He released her arm. "Stay put. I'm carrying you inside."

"Not on your life," she said, scrambling to get out.

By the time he'd rounded the car, she was leaning against it, her right ankle raised. When she looked up the moisture in her eyes glittered in the moonlight, and his heart gave an odd lurch.

"Would you . . . please help me inside, Kit?" she asked, her lips trembling.

He knew how much it cost her to have to request his help. "Of course."

"Just lend me a shoulder, all right?" she said, taking a step.

"Stop that!" he barked, pitching forward. He took her briefcase from her, then swung her into his arms again.

She didn't protest. In fact, she buried her head against his chest. "Sorry to be a bother."

"No problem," he answered her, amazed again at how tiny she felt. She couldn't weigh more than five or ten pounds over a hundred.

Sherry looped her arms around his neck and squirmed to settle more comfortably in his embrace. He carried her into her building and down the hall quickly, wanting to get a look at her foot and decide whether he should drag her to the hospital anyway. At her door, he stopped. "Keys?"

"It's not locked."

Reflexively, Kit tightened his hold on her. "What do you mean, it's not locked?"

She tipped back her head and looked up at him. "I couldn't find my keys this morning, and I had an important appointment, so . . . I didn't lock it."

"Of all the dumb, idiotic—"

"Could you at least get me inside before you yell?"

Kit shoved open the door. Kicking it closed, he carried Sherry across the living room and laid her on the couch. He inhaled, filling instantly with longing. Her home smelled like her. Sweet yet wild. Full of innocent passion.

As gently as he could, he removed her shoes. Holding one up, he commented, "If I didn't like the sight of women in these things, I'd say you're all crazy to wear them." He shook his head. "Your feet are so small, your shoes are almost as tall as they are long." He nodded at her. "Get comfortable. Take off your jacket."

She wiggled out of it, which was an enjoyable sight as her breasts thrust against the peach silk of her blouse. Once free of the jacket, Sherry winced as she rotated her ankle, testing it. "Ow."

Bending over her again, Kit lightly ran his fingers over her already-swelling ankle. "At least you can move it. That's a good sign." He straightened. "Do you have an ice pack?"

Sherry shook her head.

"I'll make do."

"Kit, you don't have to do this."

"Yes, I do."

Before leaving, he stuffed a throw pillow under her ankle, elevating it. Then, unable to resist, he stroked her cheek. "You just leave everything to Dr. Kit."

Sherry's kitchen was fairly large and airy for an apartment. She had a welcoming way of decorating. Her walls were covered in brightly woven pot holders, the butcher block island in the center of the room held ceramic salt and pepper shakers and a vase of fresh-cut spring flowers. Above the island, bright pots and pans hung side by side with cooking utensils. African violets lined the windowsill.

Kit liked Sherry's taste, and compared it to the sterile, artsy way his own place was decorated. He always hated going home. But he enjoyed being here.

He took a moment to go through all of her cabinets and drawers, to orient himself. Amazing how much they told him about the woman in the other room. She obviously enjoyed cooking, considering the wide variety of spices she kept on hand, and the amazing variety of foodstuffs in her fridge and pantry.

She was partial to dry red wine, and loved pretty ceramic things.

And she was a chocoholic. In the pantry she had bags and bags of miniature candy bars. She had chocolate ice cream in her freezer, two bottles of chocolate sauce and a jug of chocolate milk in the refrigerator, and two boxes of Cocoa Puffs stashed in a lazy Susan.

Kit grinned as he filled a cloth dishtowel with ice cubes. He'd file that information away. Maybe, someday, he'd treat her to a chocolate-covered Kit. His body liked that idea, considering its instant reaction to the erotic thought.

Taking the makeshift ice pack out to her, he arranged it gently on her ankle. "Too cold?"

"Nope, not yet."

His heart hammered as his eyes met hers. What was it about Sherry that called to his body to respond to her? He couldn't recall the last time he'd felt this quickening in his veins from merely gazing at a woman. It was almost as unnerving as it was exciting.

He pressed a quick kiss to her lips and straightened. "Be right back."

Returning to the kitchen, he started to whistle. After opening a bottle of cabernet, he grabbed it by the neck and two goblets by the stems, and started out. But abruptly he stopped and turned back. With a barely concealed grin, he snatched several small Snickers bars and stuffed them in his shirt pocket.

Inspired, he plucked a daisy from the flower arrangement, tore off half the stem and tucked it, too, into his pocket. Then he picked up the wine and glasses and headed back out to Sherry.

Pain was still etched around her pressed lips, but her eyes were open and sparkling with good humor. Another thing he liked about her, although it amazed him to realize it. He remembered his irritation at his original assessment of her as perky. She wasn't so much perky, as content with herself and the world, something so lacking in him. And for a moment, he regretted his jaded view of life. He'd give anything to be so content in his own skin.

He set the wine and goblets on the oak coffee table, then,

with a flourish, took the daisy from his pocket and presented it to her. Her mouth dropped open, forming an "o" of surprise. Before she could say anything, Kit snatched a candy bar from his pocket and waved it in the air.

She smiled. "Flowers, chocolate and wine. What more could a girl ask for?"

Immensely pleased with himself, Kit returned her smile. His facial muscles protested the unusual activity, but the rest of him felt good about it. Her grin vanished, and she stared at him as if he'd just landed a UFO in her living room.

"What?" Kit asked.

"You smiled."

"I *do* know how, you know," he retorted, feeling slightly insulted. Was he really that stuffy?

"You're just always so stuffy."

Apparently so. "Thanks a bunch."

Sherry sat up a little. "Sorry. It's just . . . I mean, you have a fantastic smile. It's such a shame to waste it."

She liked his smile? Then he'd have to start practicing. Feeling his cheeks heat up, he looked away and busied himself arranging the ice pack on her ankle. "Do you have any Ben-Gay? It might be good to put some on to help those overstretched muscles and tendons."

"Nope, no Ben-Gay."

Kit straightened. "The store across the street should have some. I'll be right back. In the meantime, you might want to take off your pantyhose."

He chanced a look at her face, and when he saw awareness flare in her eyes, he knew her thoughts had made the same leap as his. How she'd responded to him stroking her through the hose. How she had nothing on underneath the hose. How vulnerable she'd feel without them. How much he wanted to touch her without them. "You're wrong, you know," he whispered, then forced himself to smile, considering she seemed to like that a lot.

Staring at his lips, she said, "Wrong about what?"

"About why I want you." He turned and headed to the

door, deciding he'd like her to mull that one over for awhile. "Be right back."

Even Sherry's toenails were flushing with sexual heat. How was it possible for a man to make her want him with just a smile? On the other hand, what a smile it was. Kit could turn on a department store mannequin with a simple lifting of his lips, and a crinkling of his incredible eyes. The man was indecently beautiful. No one should be that lucky. So why was it so difficult for him to relax and enjoy himself? Why didn't he smile more? Why didn't he laugh? What had happened to him to turn him into such a stick-in-the-mud?

Sherry debated these questions, even as she debated taking off her pantyhose. It would be a wicked, wicked thing to do. Almost an invitation for him to try and take liberties. And after she'd figured out his motives, she shouldn't even be considering it. Oh, what the heck . . .

Working quickly, she set aside the towel and pulled off the torn hose, then shoved them under the couch cushion, finding the romance novel she'd left there weeks ago. Then she replaced the ice pack to her ankle, just as Kit returned.

Dropping gracefully to his knees, he said, "Let's take a look." He picked up the towel and leaned forward, a lock of his silky hair falling adorably over his forehead. Gingerly he touched her ankle, then snatched back his hand as if she'd burned him. Slowly, he raised his eyes until their gazes locked, and he swallowed. Hard. The tension between them was palpable, thick, and hot as sin. Sherry couldn't have taken her eyes from him if her life depended on it. Kit looked away first, still swallowing convulsively. He dropped the towel on the table and picked up the tube, mumbling under his breath.

"What?" Sherry asked.

"I was just reminding myself that you're hurt."

Not that hurt, Sherry wanted to say, but didn't. She was begging for trouble, and she knew it. Worse, she didn't care. Her lusty nature had gotten the better of her, and she realized she wanted this man beyond reason.

Sherry shut her eyes and laid her head back. At least if she didn't look at him, she wouldn't feel her hormones humming. Suddenly she felt something cool hit her ankle bone, and she flinched until she realized it was the ointment. And then with a featherlight touch, Kit began rubbing the stuff into her flesh. The coolness disappeared, and heat took its place. And not just the heat from the Ben-Gay. Unless the ointment had the power to raise her body temperature.

But no, she felt fairly certain that it was his gently massaging fingers that were responsible. And she realized that not looking at him wasn't going to stop her from responding to him. So why deny herself the pleasure?

She opened her eyes to catch him watching her face, the heat in her body reflected in his gaze. A sudden need to know him, to know what made him what he was, suffused her. "Where did you and Rachel grow up?" she asked, figuring that was about as harmless a question as she could start with.

Obviously not. The passionate fire in his eyes died as if doused with ice water, and his fingers stilled on her leg. For a moment, she felt certain he wouldn't answer her. But then he took a sip of wine, then resumed stroking her ankle. "I grew up in Allentown, Pennsylvania. Rachel grew up in Pittsburgh."

"Oh. Your parents divorced?"

Again he hesitated, his jaw clenching rhythmically. "Not exactly. My father was never in the picture."

"Oh, Kit, I'm so sorry!"

"We were separated when we were five."

"When who were five?"

"Rachel and I."

"You're . . . the same age?"

One side of his mouth quirked up. "Twins. Hard to believe, huh?"

"I've never seen two such different people."

"Yes, well, I can't argue that."

Sherry peered at him, wondering what he was leaving out. And wondering how to get him to talk. "If you didn't grow up together, which one of you lived with your mother?"

Kit stood abruptly and grabbed his goblet and the wine bottle. "I need a refresher," he said, refilling his nearly full glass. "You?"

Considering she hadn't touched her wine yet, and he'd barely made a dent in his, she saw the ploy for what it was. "If you don't want to talk about it, just tell me to mind my own business."

He opened his mouth, then closed it again. After a moment, he said, "How's your ankle feel?"

She couldn't decide whether he was too polite to tell her to stuff it, or whether some part of him wanted to talk, but he just didn't know how. "Better." She looked at his hand pointedly. "That ointment felt good."

Kit again settled on the floor near her feet. "Really? Well, now, making you feel good is my primary goal in life at the moment."

Sherry couldn't believe this potential centerfold sat on the floor at her feet, content to do her bidding. She decided to test him . . . just a little. "I'm feeling dizzy. Probably lack of chocolate in my system." His low chuckle was so deep and rumbly, Sherry popped her head up to stare at him. "What?"

"Didn't your mother teach you *it's* not polite to take advantage of people?"

"Heck, no! She took all the advantage she could get."

Kit's grin grew wider with every word. "Your mother sounds like a very intelligent woman."

"Sure is. She taught me everything I know."

"Including your flair for the dramatic?"

"You betcha. Now how about that candy bar, before I expire from chocolate withdrawal?"

Kit grabbed the chocolate bar and unwrapped it, a smile flitting over his features.

While Sherry settled herself up straighter, a little devil in her took over. "Let's make this a game."

Kit's brows lifted. "What kind of game?"

Sherry studied her nails. "Oh, I don't know. Let's see . . ."

She snapped her fingers. “I’ve got it! The queen and the slave boy.”

Eight

Kit choked.

Take that! Sherry thought. *Let's see you give up some of that infamous control, Christian Fleming.*

"Slave boy?" Kit said, still half-sputtering.

She waved. "Slave boy, slave man, whatever. It's the slave part that's important here."

His eyes narrowed. "Oh, I get it. It's the control thing again, huh?"

"Just testing. Can you possibly give it up, even for a moment?"

"Of course," he said, looking insulted. "Just watch."

He sidled toward her, still on his knees. Sherry's pulse beat faster at the mere sight of his approach. He had a wicked light in his eyes that did tremendous things to the blood in her veins.

Brandishing the small candy bar like a weapon, he leaned over her, brushing her hair back from her face. "Your wish is my command, my queen."

"I wish my candy bar," she demanded, looking imperious.

He waved the bar under her royal nose, and Sherry nearly moaned at the scent of chocolate.

"This?" he asked. "You wish this?"

"Oh, yes," she agreed, a little too eagerly for a queen.

"Ask nicely," he whispered, keeping the candy bar just out of reach.

"I'm the queen," she reminded him. "I don't have to ask. I demand."

"Ask nicely," he repeated.

"Kit, you're not playing the game right."

"Okay, since you won't ask, I now insist that you beg." He waved the candy back and forth. "Beg me, Sherry," he said.

Somehow, he'd managed to turn the tables on her. Again. Sherry wanted that candy bar badly, and he knew it. She thought about just snatching it from him, but decided maybe he needed a lesson in how to give up control. "Please."

"Please, what?"

"Please, feed me the candy bar."

"Good girl," he growled. He put the bar to her lips.

Sherry sank her teeth into the Snickers and bit off a small piece. She moaned her delight as the nectar of tastes exploded in her mouth. Nothing, *nothing,* gave her as much pleasure as chocolate. Well, maybe one thing, she amended, as she gazed at the man hovering above her. Looking at Kit was pure delight. And if just looking at him was this enjoyable, kissing him was pretty close to heaven. Complete heaven would be—

"More, my queen?" he asked.

"Yes."

"Yes, what?"

"Please," she implored softly. "Please, Kit."

Something in her voice affected Kit deeply. He felt a burn in his chest, a catch in his throat. She was so damn beautiful, so damn appealing, sitting here begging for sustenance. He could get used to this slave boy routine. He'd like to be her love slave, too, making her beg for him until they both lost their minds.

He fed her the rest of the candy, and delighted in her groan of pleasure. Oh, God, he wanted to make her moan like that while he explored her body and brought her to nirvana.

He watched her mouth move as she chewed, and couldn't wait until she swallowed so he could kiss her. He wanted to taste the sweet chocolate on her lips, her tongue.

Sherry grabbed his hand, surprising him. Before he understood what she had in mind, she'd gently sucked his index finger into her mouth. Her tongue brushed over it and he felt the sensation all the way down to his groin, which reacted in a spasm of pleasure. When she was done licking any remaining chocolate from his finger, she worked over his thumb until Kit was fully aroused.

He had to keep in mind that she was injured, and he

couldn't do what he desperately wanted to do right now—drag her to the bedroom and make love to her all night long. Use her sweet body for his satisfaction, and satisfy her in return. "Sherry," he groaned, "I want you so much."

"I hadn't noticed, slave boy," she returned, smiling.

"Notice this." He cupped her face in his hands and came down on her mouth. Explosions of sensation rocketed through his body as their tongues found each other and mated.

Just as he knew she would, she tasted so sweet, and Kit started to wonder if he'd ever tire of kissing this woman. She was so wrong about the control issue. He didn't want to make love to her just to control her. He wanted to make love to her because he desired her more than he'd ever desired a woman in his life.

Her personality, her zest for life, the very things that had irritated him when he'd first met her, now attracted him in a way he'd never dreamed possible. Sherry was the woman he wanted to make love to, the woman he wanted to share the ultimate pleasure with.

He broke the kiss and laid his forehead on hers, his breath rasping in the quiet of the room. He had to fight for control. He had to remember her ankle, and how he'd injure it further if he made love to her the way he wanted. Wildly.

But, he realized, he could give her what she wanted without hurting her. With that in mind, he tugged her down until she was lying again. Kissing her deeply, he grasped her waist, then slid his hand to the buttons of her silk blouse.

One by one, he slipped them free, working upward. He knew the minute she realized what he was doing, because she tensed. Kit lifted his head and looked down at her questioningly.

"We can't do this," she said, the regret warring with passion in her eyes.

"Why not?"

"My . . . my ankle."

He smiled at her, an action that was suddenly becoming rather easy. "For what I have in mind, your ankle will be just fine."

"What . . . what do you have in mind?"

He brushed a kiss over her lips. "Slave boy is about to pleasure his queen."

"Oh, no you don't, slave boy," Sherry said, quickly rebuttoning her shirt. "This queen doesn't allow slaves with *rules* to pleasure her."

Kit sat back on his haunches, cursing himself for ever telling her his rules. Just his luck to fall head over heels in lust for a woman with a good memory. What he should do is get up, walk out, and take the fastest route to Tiffany's hotel. He could take Tiffany up on her seductive offer, forget all about Sherry Spencer and her romantic notions. He took a sip of wine, recognizing the instant protest his body put up. The thought of intimacy with Tiffany did not turn him on. In fact, it turned him off. Way off.

He tried another tactic. "What's the matter, mistress? Afraid to let loose and live a little?"

Sherry's nose wrinkled adorably when she scoffed. "Listen, slave boy, I'm not interested in a short-term fling. I don't care how sexy you are."

Hmmm, she found him sexy. That was as good a starting point as any. "You're attracted to me. You've admitted it."

"Doesn't matter. You're all wrong for me."

Kit rolled his eyes. "Is this the romance thing again?"

"You got it. When I fall in love, it's going to be with a man who can commit. It's going to be with a man who knows the meaning of the word romance. Not some egomaniacal CEO who shudders at the mere thought of marriage."

Kit shuddered at the mere thought of marriage. Unfortunately for him, Sherry noticed. She snorted and shook her head.

He gave up. No matter how much he wanted her, he was definitely *not* the man for her. No matter how strong the sexual chemistry between them, she wanted things he couldn't give her.

He stood up, feeling bone weary. "Do you need anything before I go?"

Something flickered in her eyes, but it was gone too quickly for him to recognize what it was. She shook her head. "No, thanks. But I'm really grateful for your help tonight."

Kit stood over her, gazing at her, regret weighing him down. Damn, he wished he could give her what she wanted.

Some devilish streak he hadn't known he possessed took over. Hell, if he couldn't give her what she wanted, at least he could show her what they were missing. Why should he suffer alone?

He bent and touched her face, then kissed her. The kiss held little finesse, but it set fire to his body just the same. He hoped it would have the same effect on her. He straightened, and was pleased to see she looked stunned. "Think about *that* while you try to get to sleep tonight," he said, stifling a satisfied smirk. "Think about the pleasure this slave boy could have given you." And without giving her a chance to respond, he headed toward the door, never looking back.

"What's wrong with you these days?" Rachel asked Kit, eyeing the fork he was using to push food around his plate. "You definitely haven't been acting like yourself "

Kit bristled, because he knew exactly what was wrong with him. He couldn't stop thinking about Sherry. He couldn't stop wondering how good they could have been together.

More than a month had passed since that night in her apartment. In that time, he'd seen her several times. But this morning they'd held the screening of the first commercial, and he'd have no reason to see her again for several weeks, until they shot the second commercial. And he just knew the world was going to stand still until then. Somehow she'd managed to put them back on an emotionless, professional level. All of the desire he'd seen in her eyes the night she'd twisted her ankle had died. In fact, even the humor he'd come to enjoy had disappeared. She didn't even care enough to find him amusing.

Romance. Bah! How he'd come to hate that word. How he'd come to despise the idea that somewhere out there, at any time, Sherry might meet the man who'd give it to her. And then she'd be lost to him for good.

"Kit? Heavens, what's wrong? You're scaring me."

He looked up and shrugged. "Nothing. I've just got a lot on my mind lately."

Her brows pulled down with worry. "You're sure? I've never known you not to have a ravenous appetite."

"Is Jeff romantic?" he blurted, then seriously debated slapping himself upside the head.

Rachel's mouth dropped open. It took her a moment to answer him. "Romantic? Yes, yes, I suppose he is. Why do you ask?"

He ignored the question, looking everywhere but into her eyes. "What kinds of things does he do? Romantic things, I mean."

"Well, let's see," she said. "Sometimes he brings me jewelry for no reason."

"Jewelry," he repeated. Surely, all women loved jewelry. "What else?"

"He surprised me with that trip to Paris last year," Rachel said.

Paris. Oh, Lord, every woman's fantasy city. He supposed he could survive a trip to Paris.

"And, of course, I was in heaven when he bought me that mink." Rachel peered at him. "Why do you ask?"

Kit waved his fork, his appetite restored. "Just curious," he said, then dug into his salmon.

Sherry was having a heckuva time coming up with a good slogan for ShinyCoat dog food. Her mind just wasn't on animals. At least not the four-legged variety. Nope, her mind was firmly fixated on humans. Men. One man. One infuriating man. And had been for the last month.

Kit Fleming. The idiot. He was all she thought about, all she dreamed about. It drove her nuts, but she couldn't seem to help it. She couldn't get over that final melting kiss or his parting shot. She had, indeed, thought about him as she tossed and turned herself to sleep night after night. And she'd finally come to a horrible conclusion. She was wildly attracted to Mr. Wrong.

About the dumbest thing she could do in the world would be to have an affair with him. No matter how enjoyable, she just knew herself too well. He'd sent her to the moon just kissing her. If she ever slept with him, she'd shoot right past the moon to the sun. And she'd get burned.

Why, oh, why, couldn't he be the romantic type? What had made him so cynical? And why, knowing that whatever had happened to him had affected him permanently, couldn't she dismiss him as she wanted to? She wanted desperately to dismiss him.

Her phone rang, and she sighed with relief at the distraction.

"Sherry Spencer."

"It's Kit," the man of her nightmares said, his voice unusually gruff.

"Hello," she choked out. "What can I do for you?" She blushed just thinking about the kinds of things she'd like to do for him. To him. With him.

There was a short pause. "I need to see you. Can you meet me for dinner?"

Her heart skipped a beat just at the thought of meeting him for dinner. "Another business dinner?" she asked, stupidly hoping he was actually asking her on a date.

Another pause. "Right."

Darn. "Is it physically impossible for you to schedule business meetings outside of a restaurant?" she asked, grabbing desperately for an Almond Joy.

"I'm just . . . tied up until then." Another short silence. "Please, Sherry."

Holy cow! Kit Fleming, asking? Not demanding, not ordering, but *asking?* This was too good to be true. "Can you tell me what you want to discuss?" she responded, delaying the moment she might actually accept his invitation.

"Uhmmm, business, like I said."

"What kind of business?"

"Will you meet me for dinner, or not?"

Recognizing the impatience in his voice, Sherry sighed. "Fine. But don't be upset if I'm not prepared for whatever business you want to discuss."

"You don't need to prepare."

"Fine. Where and when?"

"I'll pick you up."

"I don't think so."

He made a growling sound that reverberated in her ear. "Fine. Meet me at the Okinawa at seven." Before she could answer him, he added, his voice strangely hesitant, "Or don't you like sushi? If you don't, we can go somewhere else."

Giving her a choice! If she weren't actually involved in this conversation, she'd never believe it of him. "Sushi's fine."

"Seven o'clock?"

"Seven it is," she agreed, almost fainting from shock.

They said their good-byes, and Sherry hung up the phone, absently munching on her candy bar. She checked her watch. Three hours away. She'd never be ready in time if she didn't hightail it out of the office now.

Tossing away the rest of the candy, she saved her file and turned off the computer. Whatever business Kit wanted to discuss, Sherry wanted to make darn sure that he couldn't help but see her as more than an ad exec.

She wanted him to see her as a woman.

Kit nearly swallowed his tongue when Sherry entered the restaurant. God, she was all woman tonight. She'd dressed in a pale pink dress that hugged her curves to magnificent perfection. Her hair was long and loose around her face, ebony silk framing delicate bones.

Why hadn't he realized just how lovely she was before? Oh, he'd always found her attractive, but right now she looked like the most attractive woman on three continents. And he wanted her so badly he burned with it.

God, he hoped this plan worked.

He stood at her approach, glaring at the man at the next

table who whistled at Sherry under his breath. "Thanks for meeting me on such short notice," he said, holding out her chair.

"No problem," she returned, smiling.

She smelled fabulous. If he didn't know better, he'd say she was dressed more for a date than a business meeting. Except for the briefcase.

He moved around to his own chair and sat, trying to decide how to proceed from here. He'd never been so nervous on a date in his life. What had happened to the cool, calculating man who remained forever in control?

He was gone. Because right now if Sherry turned those baby blues on him and told him to jump off a cliff, he'd do it without hesitation.

The waiter came, and they ordered drinks. Afterward, she treated him to a polite smile and waited, apparently content to let him get this meeting under way.

"The commercial went over well," he said, figuring that was as good a conversation starter as any.

Sherry nodded. "It's a great ad. This campaign's going to be a hit, Mr.—"

"Kit," he said sharply. "Just Kit."

"Kit."

"And it's all thanks to you," he complimented. "Your concept, your script, your . . . model."

Sherry's eyebrows shot up, but she reserved comment until the waiter served their drinks and went away. "Thanks," she finally mumbled. "I'm glad you're happy with it."

Kit took a healthy sip of his scotch. Then he set down the tumbler. "I'll get right to the point. This is how happy I am with it," he said, then pulled the envelope from his breast pocket. He laid it in front of her.

Sherry's lush mouth curved down in a frown as she picked it up. "Airline tickets?"

She flipped it open, then glanced up sharply. "Airline tickets? To *Paris?*"

"Right."

She slapped the envelope down on the table. "Look, I'm

thrilled that you liked the ad, but this is going a bit overboard, don't you think?"

Knowing he'd never be able to admit his true intent—that he wanted to attempt to romance her—he began explaining his carefully constructed excuse. "There's a company over there I'm thinking of acquiring. A perfume company. I want to take a look at it. And I was hoping you'd come along and see if you can't come up with a good marketing strategy."

She was struck speechless for a long, long minute, and Kit felt heat begin to creep up his collar to his cheeks. Finally, she cleared her throat. "Are you saying you want me to go to Paris . . . *with you?*"

"Right."

"On business?"

"Right."

She again checked the tickets. "Next week."

"Right."

She looked up and shook her head. "As much as I've always wanted to see Paris, I couldn't possibly go."

He couldn't believe the disappointment he felt. "Why not?"

"Well, number one, I've got all kinds of appointments next week."

"Cancel them."

She stared at him, then burst out laughing. "You are amazing. When are you going to learn that you're not my only client, Kit? I have other obligations."

"Okay," he said slowly. "How much time do you need to clear your calendar for a week?"

The waiter returned, and Kit started to order the deluxe sushi and sashimi platters, but stopped himself just in time to avert disaster. "Sound okay to you?" he asked Sherry.

"Fine," Sherry said, then grinned up at the waiter. "And bring lots of extra wasabi." The pale green mustard usually served with sushi was powerful stuff, but she loved it.

Five minutes later, the food arrived. Kit watched with astonished amusement as Sherry devoured the raw fish and rice rolls, slathering them with the fiery wasabi.

Watching Sherry eat was a purely sexual experience. Kit was grateful for the tablecloth that hid his reaction. The way her mouth moved filled him with an almost overpowering desire. So overpowering, he barely tasted the food himself.

"Do you want that piece of tuna?" Sherry asked, pointing a chopstick at the wooden slab filled with raw delicacies from the sea.

Kit shook his head, struck dumb. He couldn't wait to take her to every restaurant and café Paris had to offer. He thought he could watch her eat for the rest of his life. That thought brought him up short. His brain had short-circuited, obviously. "You never answered my question," he said, a little more gruffly than he'd intended. It wasn't her fault he couldn't think around her, after all.

Busy coating her tuna with wasabi, she missed his self-directed scowl. "What question was that?"

"How soon can you make it to Paris?"

Her chopsticks stilled halfway to her lips. "Look, Kit, it's really rather ridiculous for you to take me all the way to Paris for something I can do perfectly well right here. Besides, aren't you jumping the gun? You're not even certain you're buying the company."

"Oh, I'm ninety percent certain. And I want to get your thoughts."

She ate her tuna, closing her eyes in ecstasy as the wasabi was most certainly burning that sweet, sweet tongue. "I just can't see taking a week off."

Kit growled to himself. "What about vacation time? Don't you have any coming up?"

Her eyes—watering slightly from the fiery flavor—went wide. "Now what makes you think I'd want to spend vacation time working?"

This time he growled out loud. "Okay, forget the perfume thing. Just come to Paris with me."

She was about to snag a shrimp roll when her hand stilled, then slowly lowered to the table. "What the heck are you talking about? What would be the point of going, if not to do business?"

Either she was extremely dense, or she was intentionally missing the point. Either way, it aggravated the hell out of him that she was making him spell it out. "What does anyone go to Paris for?"

Definitely, she hadn't understood. Because when understanding dawned, it dawned in brilliant detail. Her look of astonishment was a wonder to behold. "You mean . . . oh, my God! I can't believe you!"

"What?" he said, wondering at her sudden outrage.

"You jerk!"

"Jerk?" he repeated stupidly, shoving a hand through his hair.

She shook her head, the outrage slowly turning to amusement. He couldn't decide which emotion bugged him more.

"You know," she said, picking up the shrimp roll. "I guess I should be extremely flattered at the lengths you'd go to, but isn't Paris an awfully expensive way to seduce a woman? I'm sure there are others out there who wouldn't expect a trip to Europe in return for going to bed with you. Seriously, dinner and a movie satisfies many of them."

It was his turn to be outraged, even if she spoke the truth. He *did* want to go to bed with her. Badly. Very, very badly. "That's not my only reason for wanting to take you there," he said, trying not to sound sulky.

"Right."

"It isn't! My sister told me that it's a great way of romancing a woman."

"Romancing?"

He pointed his chopsticks at her. "That's right! You said you wanted romance, I was trying to give it to you. I'm so happy you find the effort amusing."

She set down her chopsticks in what appeared to be a permanent manner. "That's sweet, really. And I *do* appreciate the gesture. But you don't know the first thing about romance, Christian Fleming."

"I'm trying to learn!"

"What you're talking about here is seduction. That's not the same as romance. A grand gesture, to be sure, but the wrong one. No matter what you do or say, I'm not going to go to bed with you just to satisfy your male ego."

Kit didn't think he'd ever had the urge to pout before. He had the urge now. "This isn't about my ego."

She reached out and patted his arm. "Sure it is. You can't stand the thought that there's a woman in the world who won't just fall into bed with you. I'm a challenge, that's what I am. And you hate losing." She wiped her lips on her napkin and tossed it on the table. "But don't worry, I'm flattered just the same. Well," she continued as she picked up her briefcase, "thanks for dinner."

"Don't you want dessert?" he asked desperately, not wanting her to leave, even if this dinner was becoming downright humiliating. He stood with her.

"Oh, I've already had it." She shot him a brilliant smile. "Paris. Wow, that's a new one. I love it."

And with that, she sashayed out of the restaurant.

Nine

The sable coat arrived at Sherry's office at eleven o'clock the next morning. As she pulled it from the box, she nearly choked. Dropping it on the desk, she searched through the tissue, checking for a card from the idiot.

She found it. *Sherry: Something soft and warm and the color of your hair. Enjoy. Kit*

She didn't know whether to laugh or cry. What in the world had the man been thinking? Just how badly did he want to win? First Paris, now this. The guy was an out-and-out lunatic.

She supposed she should feel flattered, but it drove her nuts that he thought he could seduce her with extravagant gifts. For just a moment she rubbed the fur against her cheek, then with a shake of her head, put it back in the box.

After calling the furrier and demanding an employee come and pick up the coat, she dialed Kit's office. Unfortunately, he was tied up in a meeting. She left a message, then hung up, slumping back in her chair.

What should she do about the man? Little did he know just how much she wanted to cave in to his seduction. She had no doubt that he'd be an incredible lover, if the expert way he aroused her with kisses alone was any indication.

Not only that, but she had gone a long time without a man. Dealing with him caused her to realize there was something big missing from her life.

But she couldn't, wouldn't let him win this one. He might supply short-term pleasure, but once he'd satisfied his own lust, he'd be gone in a hurry, leaving her to nurse a broken heart.

Because she cared about him. Probably too much already, but not nearly as much as she would if they shared intimacy. Sherry knew herself well enough to understand that fact completely.

Sex was an expression of feelings to her. An expression of trust and commitment. It might be an old-fashioned sentiment in this day and age, but it was *her* sentiment. Which meant she couldn't do what she wanted to do most in the world at the moment. Make love with Kit.

No doubt about it, she wanted him. Heaven help her, she wanted him. What sane woman wouldn't? He was gorgeous, successful, single and sexy as sin. His kisses alone could melt arctic glaciers. His touch made her flesh flame. His possession of her body would blow her mind. And make her fall in love.

She shook her head. It was a moot point. She wasn't going to bed with him, and therefore she was safe from falling in love. It was as simple as that. And wasting her time thinking about him when she had work to do was silly. She had a kitty litter ad campaign to create.

Clucking her tongue, Sherry refocused on the task at hand. But she found concentrating difficult, and her need for chocolate immense. She grabbed a Mallomar from her drawer and sat back, closing her eyes. Munching on the cookie, she tried to think of a catchy phrase that would sell kitty litter by the truckload, but nothing came to mind.

Her phone buzzed, and she quickly swallowed what was in her mouth and sat forward. "Sherry."

"Delivery man for you, Sherry," the receptionist announced.

"Good," she said, scowling at the box with the coat in it. "Send him in."

But she knew right away that this wasn't an employee from the furrier, considering the man who entered was carrying yet another package.

Sherry rolled her eyes, but kept her comments to herself. She wasn't into shooting the messenger as a rule. Smiling grimly, she took a five from her purse and handed it to the man, then waited until he left her office before tearing the paper with a vengeance. She knew who the sender was before she saw the note, but still she wasn't prepared for what was inside the wine velvet box.

Sapphires. Lots of them. Enough to form a necklace, bracelet and earrings. Sherry just stared. A month's salary couldn't have bought these baubles. The beautiful stones were all surrounded by smaller diamonds.

She snatched the card nestled under the bracelet, and dropped the jewelry box on her desk. As she opened the envelope, scathing thoughts flew through her mind. The man had more gall than the world should allow.

Sherry, these remind me of your eyes. Enjoy. Kit.

Yup, she was going to commit murder. She picked up her phone and called him. When his secretary informed her he was in yet another meeting, Sherry informed his secretary what he could do with his meetings.

Then she took a deep breath, remembering once again that this woman was blameless. "I'm sorry," she said, reaching for a package of M&M's. "Please tell Mr. Fleming it's important, and to get back to me as soon as possible."

The secretary promised, and Sherry hung up. She popped some M&M's in her mouth and ground them between her molars.

Kitty litter, Sherry. Think about kitty litter. But she couldn't. Kitty kept getting shortened to Kit. All roads led back to him. And his ridiculous courting.

Sherry suddenly grinned, her anger dissolving. The clod. Did he really think extravagant gestures would do the trick? Poor man. Poor, poor misguided man.

Her phone rang, and Sherry's heart leapt. She knew it would be Kit before she picked up. She didn't understand how she knew. She just knew. "Sherry."

"It's Kit," he said, his voice low, rumbly, and sexy as all get out.

"Well, well, well, how's tricks, Kit?"

"You tell me."

She shook her head slowly, picking up the necklace. "Kit, my man, you need help."

"Huh?"

"Do you really think I'm like all your other bimbos?"

"No," he said around a soft chuckle. "You're not a bimbo."

"Then why," she asked, her indignation growing again, "are you treating me as if I were?"

"What?"

"You have good taste, I'll have to grant you that. But if you think extravagant gifts are going to work with me, you are in for a big disappointment. Save your platinum American Express for some other girl. I can't be bought."

He growled . . . just like a tiger. "I'm not trying to buy you. I told you last night, I'm trying romance."

"Well, this brand of romance might work on other women you've kept company with, but it won't work on me."

"Dammit, Sherry! I've never tried to romance anyone before! I never had to."

Sherry's mouth popped open. The audacity of the man! "You oaf."

There was a pause. "I take it that means you're not going out with me."

"You mean go to bed with you."

"Well . . . that too."

"Adios, Kit."

"Wait, Sherry!"

"Hmmm?"

"I've tried everything I know. If you hang up now, I give up."

For some dumb reason, that made Sherry sad. But she was determined to keep her heart intact. And she knew, without a doubt, that Kit Fleming held the power to break it in two. "Give up, Kit," she said softly, then broke the connection.

"Like hell I'm giving up," Kit muttered, as he pulled into a parking space in the strip mall an hour later.

Okay, so his sister's idea of romance hadn't worked with Sherry. He probably should have known that instinctively. With Sherry, subtler gestures were called for. And since he had no idea what that meant, he'd decided to seek out advice from another source.

He entered the book-video store and looked around. It took him a moment to find the section labeled "Romance." He headed to it, feeling wildly conspicuous. But he didn't care. Sherry found something that appealed to her in romance novels, and if they held the key, he was going to read as many as he needed to find it.

Once in the romance section he stopped, and stared helplessly at the hundreds of books. How could he possibly figure out which one would give him the insight he needed to win Sherry?

He leafed through a few, but still had no idea how to decide. So he swallowed his embarrassment and sought out a clerk. "I want to talk to someone who knows something about romance novels."

Ten minutes later he left the store, two novels and a video in his possession. Unlocking his car door, he began to whistle. Sherry Spencer didn't stand a chance. Because Kit Fleming was armed and dangerous.

Sherry barely had time to register the splendor of Kit Fleming's home. She was too frantic from the phone message she'd received from him. It had started out predictably: Kit making noise about getting it right this time, and would she please give him a chance to show her. He'd been in the middle of giving directions to his house when he'd suddenly yelled, "Fire!" and then the phone had gone dead.

Her car had barely come to a halt before she was out the door and running up the majestic steps of a palatial Tudor home. The only relief she felt behind the galloping beat of her heart was that she saw no sign of a blaze out of control.

Jabbing at the doorbell and banging the heavy oak door with her fist simultaneously, she told herself no fire trucks in the driveway was a good sign. Then it hit her. No fire trucks. No smoke. No flames. No fire.

By the time the door swung open, she'd come to the suspicious conclusion that this might have been a hoax on Kit's part. And if it was, the man would soon be dead. It would be a real shame, though. He'd be the best-looking dead man she'd ever murdered.

"Sherry!" he said, and he broke into a wide grin. "Come in!"

She poked his chest, even as she followed him into his foyer. "You better tell me the back of your house is burnt to the ground, buster."

"Huh?"

"Fire!" she yelled, then pantomimed the hanging up of a phone. "Click!"

Confusion gave way to understanding, and his cheeks turned an interesting shade of embarrassed. "Oh, yeah, that. I . . . had a bit of an accident."

"What's that smell?" she asked, as a horrifying scent assaulted her. "That's not burnt chocolate, is it?" A hoax was worthy of censure. Ruining chocolate ranked right up there with a few of the seven deadly sins.

His neck turned even brighter red. "I didn't do it on purpose! It was my first attempt. Besides, I was cooking them for you!"

"Cooking what?" she asked, dreading the answer.

"Double fudge brownies."

She didn't know whether to laugh or cry. On the one hand, what a sweet gesture. On the other hand, she mourned the death of the poor brownies. But right then the foyer actually snagged her attention. "My God, Kit," she whispered.

He glanced around. "Like it?" he asked.

"I guess it'll have to do," Sherry said dryly, but when she saw the disappointment flash in his eyes she added, "It's beautiful, Kit. Truly."

"It needs work. Want a tour?"

Heck, yes, she wanted a tour. But she was still just irritated enough that he'd managed to shave about a decade off her life. She shrugged casually. "I suppose, since I'm already here."

Kit's house did not need work. Kit's house was perfect.

Perfectly decorated, perfectly clean, perfectly . . . sterile.

The huge marble foyer led off in several intriguing directions and Kit took her in every one: to a completely white living room, completely brown den, completely antique library, completely formal dining room. The kitchen was the industrial variety, fully equipped to prepare meals for legions. At least that's what she gathered through the smoke.

"You live here alone, do you?" Sherry asked, wondering why one man would want this much space.

"I have a housekeeper," Kit answered her, sounding defensive.

"No doubt."

They returned to what Kit called his informal living room, probably the only room on the first floor that Sherry found pleasant. The overstuffed couch, love-seat and chairs were all hunter green leather, the Persian rugs worn but lovely. At the far end of the room one step led up to a raised platform which held a baby grand piano. Behind the piano was a set of French doors, leading out to a patio, and a huge lawn beyond.

"Now this room I like," Sherry murmured to herself.

Kit turned to her, his brows raised. "You don't like the rest of the house?" he asked, his tone slightly injured.

She laid a hand on his arm. "I didn't mean that. I meant . . . well, just that—"

"It feels like no one lives here."

That was exactly what it felt like. There were no personal touches anywhere. They could be strolling through a model home. "Well, you're a busy man."

"You're a busy woman, but your place feels like a home."

Sherry looked up in surprise. She wouldn't have thought Kit capable of making an observation like that. Suddenly she realized her hand was still on his arm. The heat from his body seeped through his cotton polo shirt to warm her clear to the core. She let her hand drop away reluctantly. Quite frankly, she enjoyed touching this man much too much. "Women are better at that sort of thing," she said, not knowing what else to say.

His hand raked through his hair. "Yeah, I guess so," he

muttered, but didn't sound convinced.

"Well, I better get going."

"No!" he said, then quickly added, "I was in the middle of inviting you to supper when the brownies self-destructed. Will you stay?"

She shouldn't. Being near this man was not good for her peace of mind. On the other hand, it was Saturday night, and the most exciting plans she had for the evening involved giving herself a mud facial. What could it hurt? *Plenty,* a voice inside her said. She ignored it. She was far too intrigued at the idea that Christian Fleming, CEO, and romance-challenged superstud, had gone to all this trouble on her behalf. "What's for supper? I'm starved."

He grinned down at her, causing Sherry's breath to catch in her throat. When this man decided to smile, he did it with a vengeance. He spread his arms, bowing slightly. "Let the games begin."

She laughed. "What's the occasion?"

Kit tapped the tip of her nose lightly. "I'm about to prove to you that I can be as romantic as the next guy."

Her grin disappeared as she stared up at him. "You are?" she squeaked.

"Yes, ma'am," he said, his smile fading as his eyes took on a smoky gleam.

Oh, Lord, she was in trouble. Her biggest defense against Kit was her knowledge that he was a slug in the romance department. If he did a good job, her defenses would fall like a house of cards.

"Sherry?" he whispered, his knuckles grazing over her cheek.

"Hmmm?"

The pad of his thumb whispered over her lower lip. "You are a beautiful woman," he said softly. "A very beautiful woman."

Her emotional house of cards collapsed.

Ten

"Just wait here," Kit told Sherry, settling her on the love seat after pouring her an ice-cold beer.

For some reason, she still seemed dazed. Hadn't anyone ever told her she was beautiful before? He found that difficult to believe.

Her lips haunted his dreams, her eyes were so lovely he could look into them forever. She was petite, yet her curves were there, in all the right female places. Even her hands, so small and soft and vulnerable, called to something elemental within him. He wanted those hands on his body so badly, his nerve endings jangled with it.

He moved outside through the French doors and sniffed the summery air. He'd fix that. Autumn scents were the romancy kind. At least according to the first novel he'd read.

He strolled to the roasting pit in his backyard. The dead leaves and twigs he'd gathered earlier still lay in a pile. With a disposable lighter he set off little fires all around the pile, blowing on them to help spread the flames. When he had a good blaze going, he waved his arms through the smoke, trying to scent the air around the pit. Satisfied, he returned to the house. Sherry still sat where he'd left her, seeming lost in thought. She looked up absently as he pulled the door closed.

Kit held up a finger. "I need to get a few things. Wait right here."

He strode out of the room and headed for the kitchen pantry, where Mrs. Fabbersham had left the picnic basket. Grabbing the cooler from the refrigerator, he carried it and the basket back to Sherry.

She arched a brow at him. "A picnic?"

"Yup," he said, just about bursting with pride. *Thank you,*

Judith McNaught, he thought, acknowledging the romance writer as the source of his inspiration.

"Come with me, young lady," he said. "And bring our mugs."

Sherry dutifully got to her feet, a twinkle of anticipation in her eyes.

They stepped outside, and Kit stopped her on the veranda. "Take a deep breath. What do you smell?"

Sherry breathed in, and then her eyes closed in appreciation, a smile lighting her face. "Burning leaves."

"Right!" Kit boasted. "What does it remind you of?"

Her eyes opened, and she gifted him with an expression of such pure enjoyment, his breath caught. Why had he never done this before? Why had he never realized the benefits of giving a woman a little romance? It really wasn't all that difficult, and the results were well worth it.

"It smells like autumn," Sherry whispered.

"Good girl, you get an A." He nodded toward the pit. "Come on."

The barbecue pit sat just at the edge of his yard, adjacent to the woods. When they reached it, it was still smoking, but most of the leaves had burned to ash. Kit set down the basket and cooler, then added some more kindling to the smoldering pile until he had a good little campfire going.

Sherry stood silently, glancing around his grounds, sipping her beer on occasion. God, she filled out a pair of jeans like no woman he'd ever seen before. The denim hugged her slightly rounded bottom so beautifully it made his mouth water just to look at her from behind.

He couldn't wait to get his hands on that luscious rump. He couldn't wait to get his hands on every inch of her naked, warm, silky flesh. But right now he had to practice patience, show her he was worthy of the honor.

He prayed she'd find him worthy of the honor.

"Can I help you with anything?" Sherry asked.

"Nope," he said, rocking back on his heels. "This is my party."

He pulled a bright red blanket from the large basket and shook it out. He laid it alongside the pit, then sat down. He patted a space beside him with one hand and reached out for his beer mug with the other.

Sherry sank to the blanket beside him and handed him his beer. Even over the fragrance of the fire, he could smell her fresh, enticing scent.

"So far, so good?" he asked, tucking a lock of her hair behind her ear. His fingertips brushed its shell, and he felt the jolt of awareness through every inch of his body. He caressed her earlobe between his fingers, and watched as her blue eyes went dark and limpid. He forgot he'd even asked her a question, until she said softly, "So far, so good."

He bent and took her mouth, cupping her neck. It was a slow, leisurely kiss, but still it managed to make his heart beat frantically, his loins tighten painfully.

The strength of his response reminded him that he hadn't had sex in a good long time. Not since . . . he'd met Sherry. He hadn't even dated other women in that time. His thoughts, his focus had been solely on this one since the first moment he saw her. And here she was, kissing him with a tender ardor that made him ache.

And not just ache with sexual need, although she turned him on to record proportions. But there was another kind of ache she brought on. An ache in his chest that he was hard-pressed to explain.

Kit broke the kiss, lifting his head. He stared down at this woman who affected him so deeply, wondering where all this would lead. Well, besides to bed. But then he shoved the question aside, not wanting to analyze something that had always seemed basically simple. He was a man, she was a woman, and there was a strong sexual chemistry between them. Logical reasoning would have him conclude that those facts would lead to them making love. After that, he didn't want to think. He smiled into her dreamy eyes. "I love kissing you."

"You do?" she asked, her voice a husky whisper.

"I do."

Swallowing, she said, "Likewise."

He thought of lying her down, right here, taking off her clothes and making love. This minute. This second. He wanted to, more than he wanted to take his next breath. But he prided himself on his timing. On enjoying the anticipation as much as the conquest. So he turned and pulled the cooler to them and took out another beer. Twisting the top, he lifted it. "Refill?"

Sherry looked a little off balance, as if his change of direction confused her. She shook her head as if to clear it and held out her mug.

After refreshing both their beers, Kit stretched out his legs and crossed his ankles, realizing with a start that this was exactly where he wanted to be, and she was exactly the person he wanted to be with. If he remembered correctly, with the other women in his life, his thoughts often strayed to other places, other events. Right now, he was all consumed with the woman beside him. Possibly because he'd never met one he enjoyed spending time with as much.

"This is really nice, Kit," Sherry said, staring up at the darkening sky.

"Enjoying yourself?" he asked, inordinately pleased.

"Very much."

"Good."

He set down his mug, grabbed two of the longer sticks from the pile beside the pit, then pulled a small knife from the picnic basket.

"What are you doing?" Sherry asked.

"Carving our cooking utensils."

"You mean . . . oh, Kit, please tell me we're having a weenie roast!"

"We're having a weenie roast."

She squealed her delight, scrambling to her knees. "I haven't been to a weenie roast since Girl Scout camp."

Kit glanced over at her. "Girl Scout camp. That figures."

"What figures?" she asked, her grin fading.

"That you went to camp. You had a perfect childhood, didn't you?"

She tilted her head, seeming to ponder it. "I don't think there's any such thing. But, yes, I had a happy childhood."

"You said you have an older brother."

She smiled softly, obviously very fond of her brother. "Yes. Mark."

"I take it he didn't boss you around as a kid, huh?"

Her laughter warmed his heart. "Of course he did." She tossed her braid over her shoulder. "But I got him back. Whenever he tried to tell me what to do, I'd threaten to tell his girlfriends about each other."

Kit grinned. "Ah, blackmail. Effective. Another technique learned from your mother?"

"You got that right."

Shaking his head in amusement, he felt a sense of contentment settle inside him. He liked hearing about Sherry's life as a child. "Let me guess. You got straight A's, you dated the captain of the football team, you were homecoming queen, and you were a cheerleader. Am I right?"

Before he'd met Sherry, he'd have said that derisively. But with her, things felt different. He *wanted* to hear all that.

Sherry chuckled. "I was first runner-up for homecoming queen, and I dated the captain of the soccer team. Otherwise, you're dead on." She took a healthy slug of beer. "Am I that predictable?"

Kit started sharpening the second stick. "Not predictable. Just . . . I don't know, comfortable with yourself. Confident." His pitch lowered. "Happy."

"I guess I'm happy. Although, I haven't accomplished everything I want in life, not by a long shot."

He set down the second stick and glanced at her. It had grown dark enough that they needed the illumination of the fire to see one another. The light from the flames danced over her face, as if highlighting one adorable feature at a time. It glowed around her, making her appear somewhat ethereal. "What else do you want, Sherry?"

She hugged her knees to her chest. Staring into the fire, she said, "Well, I guess I dream the usual dreams. Falling in love, getting married, starting a family."

Kit's heart pinched painfully. He swallowed some beer before commenting. "Of course." He reached out and brushed hair from her cheek. "You want to hear something funny?"

"What?"

"For the first time in my life, I'm sorry I'm not capable of fulfilling a woman's dreams. You make me wish . . ." His voice trailed off.

She sucked in an audible breath. "You're sure about that, are you?"

Kit busied himself spearing a hot dog on each stick, then he handed one to Sherry and held his over the open flame. "Very sure."

"Why, Kit?" she asked, adding her weenie to the fire. "What happened to you when you were younger?"

A painful drumbeat began in his chest. He considered not answering her, but then changed his mind. If nothing else, she deserved an answer. "When Rachel and I were five, our mother made the decision to give us up for adoption."

"Oh, no!"

"It wasn't her fault!" he said quickly. "She didn't have any choice. She just couldn't take care of us."

"I'm sure. I can't imagine a mother taking that drastic a measure unless she's run out of choices," Sherry said.

The understanding in her voice caused his throat to tighten. "Anyway, Rachel and I went to different foster homes. Within a year she was adopted by a wonderful family. She had a childhood much like yours." He twirled his hot dog to char the other side. "In fact, you remind me of her in some ways. Happy with yourself."

"And you're not? Happy with yourself, I mean?"

He shook his head. "Not in the same way. I mean, I'm proud of some of my accomplishments. I worked my way through college, and I climbed the corporate ladder at a pretty fast clip."

He drank more beer before getting on with the painful part. "But I wasn't as lucky as Rachel. My foster family was a nightmare. My foster mother and father couldn't stand each other. Or any of the kids they took in, for that matter. Why they did it, I'll never know." He took a breath. "Mr. Howard was a drunken bully, who liked nothing better than tormenting his foster kids. The more defiant we were, the more he abused us."

"And let me guess, you were a defiant young man."

"I was a defiant young man," he agreed.

"And Mrs. Howard?"

Kit snorted. "She didn't mind defiance. She minded happiness. She couldn't stand to see us laugh, smile, play. If she caught us enjoying ourselves, she'd assign a disgusting chore to wipe the smiles off our faces. If she had to be miserable, she wanted to make sure she had company."

"Oh, Kit!"

His laughter was tinged with bitterness. It was a horrible sound, even to his own ears. "So you see, my role models weren't the best. I decided a long time ago that I'd never get myself trapped in a situation like that as long as I lived. It was a conscious choice then. Now it's just . . . ingrained, I guess. I don't have whatever it takes."

"You could learn."

"No," he said, looking directly in her eyes to make sure she understood the truth of what he was saying. He respected her enough to give her that. "I know myself too well. I don't have whatever gene rules that part of a person. It's just not there for me."

Sherry's heart was crying. It explained so much. His bleak expressions, his rusty laughter, his need to be free. Most especially, his need to be in control.

During the important years, he'd been at the mercy of two unhappy human beings, and it had colored his world. He hadn't been taught to love and accept love. Romantic love was a completely foreign emotion to him.

And though it hurt more than it should to realize that he never *could* be the man she wanted to spend the rest of her life with, at least she respected his honesty. He was telling her up front what his limitations were.

In that sense, he'd relinquished control. If she told him to take a hike this minute, he'd do it without hesitation. If she told him she never wanted to see him again outside of business, he'd agree.

Though Kit was obviously attracted to her, wanted her, he could never love her. She ached for him, ached for herself. Under other circumstances, he'd be everything she was looking for. And if he weren't so jaded, if the pain of his childhood didn't tarnish every aspect of his life, she might have found a way to help him heal.

But he didn't want to heal. He wanted that pain to wrap around him as a shield against ever feeling it again. So he couldn't give her what she wanted. But perhaps, at least in a small way, she could give him what he needed.

She set aside her stick and turned to him. "Kit?"

"Yes?" he answered, without looking at her.

"I'm not hungry any longer."

Then he did turn to her, and the glimmer in his eyes was about equal parts panic and regret. "You . . . want to leave?"

She shook her head. "I want you to take me to bed."

His eyes went wide. "What?" he whispered, in a raw rasp.

"You heard me."

"Sherry, it . . . it won't change anything. You have to know that before anything happens between us."

"I know it."

"I mean, I want that, too. You have no idea how much I want that."

"Good. Then what's the problem?"

He followed her lead and abandoned his hot dog. Plowing both hands through his hair, he stared bleakly into the fire. "I'd never forgive myself if I hurt you. I . . . I like you a lot. I respect you."

"I'm going into this, eyes wide."

"Oh, God!" he said, dropping his forehead to his knees.

She touched his shoulder, and he flinched. "What's wrong?" she asked, feeling a little swell of panic herself. Here she sat offering him exactly what he wanted, and he seemed to be changing his mind.

"Sherry." He whispered her name like a caress. "You deserve better than this. You deserve better than me."

"This is my choice to make. I've made it."

He swiveled his head and gazed at her. "I've wanted this for so long, can't remember what my life was like before I started dreaming of it. Dreaming of you. But now, I don't know if I can—"

"You can," she said with a slight smile. "I have every confidence in you."

He moved so swiftly, Sherry didn't have time to react. Before she could even gasp, he'd turned to face her and hauled her to her knees, clutching her shoulders. "Tell me you won't regret this."

"I won't," she said, with much more confidence than she felt.

"Tell me you won't hate me when it's over."

That one she could promise much more easily. Although she knew she was taking a big risk, she also knew she could never hate the tortured man before her. "I won't hate you, Kit."

A low moan passed through his lips. "I don't think I've wanted anything more in my life. I want you so much it's killing me."

"I'm all yours, Christian Fleming."

He breathed a curse word before yanking her against him. Staring down at her, he made promises with his eyes that stole her sanity. No promises of forever, just of the here and now. He was giving her this moment, and Sherry knew it had to be enough.

Deliberately, she tugged his shirt from his jeans. He raised his arms, and she pulled it up and off, then tossed it aside. "Oh, Kit," she whispered at her first glimpse of his bare chest. It was breathtakingly beautiful, with a light sprinkling of golden brown hair. His shoulders were wide and powerful, his flesh smooth, his ribs and abdominal muscles rigidly defined.

She laid her hands on his chest, feeling his incredible heat. Her palms slid upward as she reveled in touching him.

"Sherry," he murmured, his eyes sliding shut. "I'm . . . dying, here."

"You are very much alive."

Sherry's husky laughter floated on the warm midsummer breeze. Excited beyond her wildest imaginings, she let all of her misgivings melt into nothing but raw, aching need. She cupped his jaw, loving the raspy feel of his day-old growth of beard. Then her hands dropped to his leather belt.

He grabbed her wrists, opening his eyes. "My turn." With deliberately slow movements, he unbuttoned her blouse. Tossing it onto his shirt, he immediately slid her bra straps from her shoulders, letting them dangle at her upper arms.

He bent his head, and worshipped the hollow of her shoulder, sending chills of delight racing through her. His lips traveled up her neck to her ear, and he gently bit at the lobe. His hands skimmed over her shoulders, then down to her shoulder blades, and he worked the clasp until she felt it snap open.

"I love the way you smell," he said. "I'll never forget your scent as long as I live." He pulled her bra from her arms and tossed it aside. He swallowed hard as his gaze devoured her naked breasts. "I knew it. Oh, God, I knew."

In one swift move, he lifted her up and laid her down, then fell beside her, taking a breast into his mouth. Sherry arched up with a cry as the sensation rocked her. Not just the tugging pull from his lips, but the tickling of her skin where his hair had fallen forward to whisper over it.

Sherry pressed his head against her as a pulsing began deep in her belly. "Hurry, Kit. Please, hurry," she pleaded.

"No way," he growled. "I want this to last." But he did start to remove her shoes, jeans and panties. When he'd finished he sat back and just stared at her. Every inch of her.

His gaze was so filled with awe she knew no embarrassment. She bent a knee, and reached for his belt once more. "Your turn again," she whispered.

While she unbuckled, he removed his wallet from his back pocket and took out a handful of foil packets. Sherry almost laughed. If they used them all, they might be there for a week.

Kit stood just long enough to get rid of the rest of his clothing, and Sherry fairly gaped as she soaked in the vision of him in his entirety. He was magnificent. And for tonight, he was all hers. "Come here," she demanded.

Kit quickly joined her, pulling her into his arms. For a long, lingering moment they lay body to body, flesh to flesh, male to female. Her aching breasts pressed into his ribs, and she squirmed a little to relieve the pressure.

Kit groaned, then pulled back. "Lord, Sherry, I've never seen anyone so beautiful."

And suddenly his hands were everywhere, skimming over her body in erotic strokes, making her quiver with ecstasy. She'd never felt this way before, as if she would die if she couldn't draw him inside her soon. She needed him to possess her more than she'd ever needed anything in her life.

Her fingers roamed over his torso, marveling at the muscle and sinew just below the surface of his skin. He was a powerful man, and she wanted to reduce him to a trembling mass of need, just as he was doing to her.

She reached for him, but he quickly stayed her wrist, forcing her arm over her head. Then he did the same with the other, as he straddled her hips. Leaning over her, he kissed her thoroughly, until she shook with her desire.

He lifted his head and gazed down at her, his eyes glittering green in the firelight. His hair fell over his forehead and looked adorably sexy. "How much do you want me?" he asked in a raw whisper.

"Terribly."

As he lowered his head, he smiled. "It won't be terrible, Sherry. I promise you that."

"Oh, I know," she moaned. "I know."

His lips traveled down her body, exciting her to a pitch she'd never reached before. When his tongue circled her bellybutton, she cried out. "Please," she started chanting, the words coming out in breathless puffs. "Please, please, please."

His mouth moved back up to her breasts, first one, then the other, while his fingers started probing her below. Sherry cried out again as he caressed her, making her slick with wanting him.

"Now, Kit. Now."

He sat up and grabbed a condom, tearing the foil savagely with his teeth. He rolled it into place, then stared at her for a long moment before positioning himself above her. "What do you want?" he asked.

"You."

"Where?"

"Inside me, over me . . . everywhere."

He thrust into her then, and Sherry emitted a sharp cry at the initial stab of pain. He went dead still, staring at her in horror. "Oh, my God! You're a—"

"No," she interrupted, as the pain subsided, and all she felt was a tingling of need. Of aching unfulfillment she needed him to address. "I'm not. It's just been a long time."

"I'm sorry," he whispered. "I'm so sorry."

"Do . . . it," she gritted out, so close to losing her mind. "Take me."

Slowly, tentatively, he began a gentle rocking motion, which did more to heighten her need than slake it. She wrapped her legs around his hips, and grasped his hard buttocks, demanding more. Or begging for more. She didn't know which any longer.

"Harder," she demanded hoarsely. "I'm not a china doll."

Kit complied, stroking into her harder, faster and deeper. And just as she thought she couldn't take it anymore, she reached her climax, rolling through her in overwhelming waves.

She screamed. His name.

Just as the incredible sensation began to subside, Kit thrust into her once, twice, three times, grinding out the words, "This . . . feels . . . so good."

Her fingernails dug into the damp flesh of his back as she felt his arousal pulse inside her, and her climax began again.

She screamed. His name. Again.

"Sherry, Sherry, Sherry," he gasped as he continued to thrust into her, drawing out her pleasure.

Finally he slowed, then stopped and buried his head against her neck, his breaths hot and fast against her sensitive flesh. The muscles in his back eased under her fingertips.

For a long, long time they held each other, both trying to recover. For Sherry, she knew no amount of time would ever be enough. She'd never recover from this.

Because she'd fallen in love with him.

Eleven

She'd fallen in love with him.

Sherry squeezed her eyes shut as the horrible realization dawned on her. She'd gone and done what she'd promised herself she wouldn't do. She'd neatly tied up her heart in ribbons of love, and handed it to him.

Kit pushed up to his elbows and gazed down at her, the sensual satisfaction in his eyes magnificent to behold. She didn't remember any man looking at her like that. Ever.

Her throat closed up. There were no words, except the ones he didn't want to hear. She blinked the swimming moisture from her eyes.

"Hey!" he whispered. "Why the tears?" Then he went stiff. "I hurt you."

Oh, God, yes. He'd hurt her, but not in the way he thought. And she couldn't even blame him, because he'd warned her from the beginning. She blinked again, and gave him a shaky smile. "No, you didn't."

"Are you sure?"

Still joined, he rolled them over, until she lay straddled on top of him. She put her hands on his chest and sat up straighter. Immediately his eyes went to her breasts, and he audibly gulped. "Damn, Sherry, you're something else."

"Something else," she repeated, not feeling particularly else-like. No indeed, she was the same Sherry, a woman for whom love and sexuality were inextricably combined. She didn't have it in her to make love and walk away.

But this time, she *would* walk away. Not for her own sake, surely, but for Kit's. He'd made her promise she wouldn't take their lovemaking more seriously than that, and as far as she was concerned, she would keep that promise, at least on the outside.

She loved him that much. She conjured a wan smile from the bottom of her bruised soul. "Thank you, Mr. Fleming, for keeping your promise."

One brown brow arched, and he shot her a lazy smile, while his fingers traced her hip bones. "What promise was that?"

Her sweet smile brightened. She was determined to keep things light, no matter how much it hurt. "Well, I wasn't really sane at the time, but I could swear I might have let out a short squeal or two there."

His chuckle rumbled through her. "Lady, you scared the birds out of the trees."

"Did I scare you?"

His smile deepened. "Not hardly. You drove me wild with it."

She bent down and folded her arms over his chest, crushing her breasts against him. "Yup, you're a wild man all right."

Kit groaned. "You wouldn't believe what you do to me."

She stifled a sob, because what she wanted to do with him would never happen. But she had tonight, and she fully planned on making the most of it. If she couldn't have the man for the rest of her life, she'd at least have her memories. Small compensation, but the best she'd get.

"Let's do it again," she whispered, brushing her lips over his.

His hands slid up her back, and gooseflesh rose in their wake. She shivered.

"Are you cold, sweetheart?"

The endearment was almost the last straw. It wasn't the first time he'd called her that, but the sentiment now meant more than it should. More than he intended it to mean. She shook her head. "It's a warm night."

"Then why are you shivering?"

"I . . ." Her voice caught, and she cleared her throat. "I like your hands on me."

"That's good, because I plan on having them on you a lot tonight."

Tonight. Since Sherry was close to breaking down, which

she didn't want him to witness, she held his handsome face and kissed him deeply. He responded instantly, his hands tightening on her waist as he rocked his lower body upward.

The kiss turned frantic. Sherry couldn't get close enough to him, couldn't draw him in deep enough so she'd never have to let him go.

Abruptly he lifted her off him, his breaths ragged. She started to protest, but he held up a hand. "I have business to take care of first, sweetheart. Just give me a minute."

She watched, fascinated, as he took care of protection. He seemed somewhat amused by her unblinking absorption in the task.

"Sherry?" he said, as he disposed of the used condom.

"Hmmm?"

"Take a look in the picnic basket. There's something in there that might interest you."

Reluctantly she dragged her gaze from him and pulled the basket closer. Searching through the contents, a smile tugged at her lips. "You have the makings for s'mores."

"Yup, but that's not what I'm talking about."

Brow furrowed, she dug deeper. Then suddenly, she burst out laughing, as she pulled a bottle of Hershey's Syrup from the basket. Glancing up, she caught him smiling at her in a way that almost made her heart explode. "What?"

"I like making you laugh," he admitted quietly. "Your laughter's as pretty as the rest of you."

The guy didn't know it, but for a completely unromantic fool, he sure said the sweetest things on occasion. "Thank you."

"No, thank *you*," he replied, leering at her. He held out his hand. "Okay, hand it over."

She drew back. "Nope."

His smile transformed into a look of consternation. "No?"

Sherry shook her head, then pushed him down to his back. Tossing aside the bottle of syrup she said, "Who needs chocolate? I want you raw."

His uncertainty shone in his troubled eyes. "I … don't know."

"Afraid to give up the dominant position?"

"Well . . . a little."

Sherry was surprised by his admission. But then she realized she shouldn't have been. He'd made several admissions tonight that had to have been painful. She lay down next to him on her side. "Let go, Kit," she said softly. "Just lie back and let me love you this time."

"I—I've never—"

She bent over him and swiped her tongue over his nipple. He sucked in a noisy breath. "God, Sherry," was all he said, but there was a tone of surrender in those two words.

When Sherry woke up, she realized she was in a bed. Early morning light came through the window, bathing the room in a reddish-gold glow. She stretched, and every muscle she owned protested, a pleasurably painful reminder of the previous night.

Kit's scent was everywhere, filling her with delight. Lord, she loved his masculine fragrance. She rolled over, fully expecting him to be in bed beside her. But he wasn't. Disappointment replaced delight, but she shrugged it off. She'd just spent the most wonderful night of her life.

She fluffed her pillow and then the extra one, inhaling deeply the subtle tang of Kit's aftershave. Stacking them, she lay back, arms thrown over her head, as she relived every incredible moment.

They'd made love so many times she'd lost count. Time had hung suspended as they'd taken turns worshipping each other. She'd never felt so treasured, so cherished.

And then, sometime in the night, she'd become drowsy, and had yawned widely. He'd grinned down at her, then tucked her into the crook of his shoulder. His fingers had stroked through her hair, over and over, in a gentle, delicious rhythm that had lulled her into a peaceful sleep.

At some point he must have picked her up and carried her to the house, because she didn't remember walking—

"Oh, my God," she whispered, as hazy memories started

taking shape in her head.

"It's getting chilly out here, sweet," she somehow thought he'd murmured in her ear. "Let's go inside."

"Too comfy," she believed she'd mumbled.

Vaguely she remembered being lifted into strong arms. Vaguely she remembered looping her hands behind his neck and snuggling against his warm, broad chest. Vaguely she remembered his steady gait, as he carried her inside. Vaguely she remembered him tucking her in bed, and telling her he'd be back as soon as he brushed his teeth. Vaguely she remembered voicing a groggy protest.

Then, as clear as the night sky that had enveloped them, she remembered burrowing deeper into the bed and whispering, "Kit?" And when he'd answered her, she'd said, "I love you."

"Oh, no!" she said aloud now, covering her eyes with her hands. "I didn't. I couldn't. I wouldn't." But she had.

She remembered now. She remembered the utter stillness that had suddenly cloaked the room. She remembered being surprised by it. And then she remembered falling into a contented void.

She'd told him she loved him. Good Lord, no wonder he'd stayed away from his own bed. With a guilty pang, she wondered if he'd had to sleep on the couch, or on a guest bed. She'd driven him away.

Heart pounding, she pushed up from the bed and got to her feet. In horror she realized she was still naked. Glancing frantically around the room, she tried to locate her clothes, without success.

Running to the bathroom, she quickly splashed water on her face, then brushed her teeth, praying he wouldn't mind her stealing a brand-new toothbrush from his medicine cabinet.

Then she returned to the master bedroom and tried to decide what to do. No way would she climb back into bed and wait for him to bring her clothes. In truth, what she wanted to do was sneak out of the house and avoid the confrontation she knew was brewing.

Well, what had he expected? How could he make love to

her the way he had, and not expect her to fall in love with him? No one, *no one* had ever loved her like that.

Biting her lower lip, she walked to what she assumed was his closet door and opened it. Naturally it was a walk-in the size of her bedroom. Switching on the light, she took inventory. The man owned enough clothes to open a store.

Grimly, she chose the first white shirt she saw and put it on. The sleeves hung well past her fingers, so she rolled them up. The tails of the shirt nearly reached her knees, but the slits on the sides exposed plenty of thigh.

Well, that couldn't be helped. She certainly couldn't borrow a pair of pants. They'd just fall to her ankles, anyway. Besides, there wasn't an inch of her he didn't know. Didn't know very, very well.

Dread clogged her throat, but she managed to open the door just the same. She walked down a long hallway to the winding staircase. Peering down over the banister, she searched for Kit. All she saw was a huge marble foyer.

Gingerly, she made her way down the stairs, for some reason reluctant to make a sound. As she neared the first floor, the tantalizing aroma of fresh-brewed coffee hit her, and her stomach rumbled. What she wouldn't give for a Snickers bar right now.

At the bottom of the steps she stopped. Then, steeling herself, she raised her chin, stiffened her spine, and followed the smell of coffee. At the door to the kitchen she stopped. The master of the house was sitting at the broad oak table, staring into his mug, a brooding, bleak expression on his face. He looked like he hadn't slept all night. His hair was in adorable disarray, as if some woman had spent the night threading her fingers through it. Which, of course, some woman had. His beard was heavier and fatigue lines creased his forehead.

Yup, she'd definitely told him she loved him.

She couldn't see what Kit wore on the lower half of his body, but his upper half was decidedly bare. And beautiful. Bathed in the early morning light streaming in through the window, his skin glowed golden.

"Good morning," Sherry said, trying to sound cheerful. Trying not to sound like she knew her heart was about to be broken. Maybe if she just pretended not to remember, they could both ignore what she'd said.

Lord, she needed a chocolate fix.

His head snapped up as if she'd startled him. He took in her attire in one quick sweep, then his eyes began darting around the room. "Did you . . . sleep well?"

She strolled into the room, ignoring the agitated tic in his jaw. "Don't remember. I was unconscious at the time." She tugged at the hem of his shirt. "Sorry about this, but I couldn't seem to locate my own clothes."

His gaze again traveled over her, and though his expression seemed bleak, something flared in his eyes. "I washed them. They're in the dryer now."

"Oh! Well, thank you."

"You're welcome."

Sitting down across from him, she asked, "You?"

"What?"

"How'd you sleep?"

He swallowed. "I wasn't tired."

She decided not to call him the lousy liar he was. "May I have some coffee?"

He jumped to his feet so quickly Sherry nearly started crying. Obviously, the man was nervous, and he didn't know how to handle her declaration of love. Unfortunately, she knew how she had to handle it. And her heart began splintering apart at the realization.

Another realization hit her. Kit wore nothing except paisley silk boxers. And he looked fantastic in paisley silk boxers. The muscles in his arms and back rippled with his movements, and his butt filled out those boxers in a very attractive way.

He brought her a steaming mug, and waved at the cream and sugar on the table. She added a generous amount of both, then drank, closing her eyes in appreciation.

Kit prowled the large kitchen, seeming unable to sit still with her in the room. Sherry set down her mug and sighed. It was time to get to the point. "Thanks for putting me to bed."

He stopped at the sink and looked out the window. "You're welcome."

"Kit?"

"Yes?"

"Please come here."

Reluctance was written in every dragging step he took toward the table. He sat down and again stared into his mug. His hair fell over his forehead and impatiently he shoved it back.

"Kit?"

"Yes?"

"Look at me."

He raised his head.

"Are you always this charming the morning after?"

He blinked. "Excuse me?"

"Are you regretting last night?"

His mouth dropped open. "How can you even ask a question like that?"

"Pretty easily, when you're acting like I'm some kind of disease you'd rather not contract."

His coffee mug hit the table with a dull thud. "I am not."

"Look at yourself," she said, waving. "You're afraid to look at me, and if I walked around this table right now, you'd probably jump up and run."

His head dropped forward and his fingers massaged his temples. "It's not you, Sherry."

"Then what is it?"

He sipped his coffee before answering, whether as a stall tactic or to help him get his thoughts together, she didn't know. Finally, he stood and went to the coffee maker, refreshing his cup. "More coffee?"

"No, thank you."

After pouring, he turned back to her. "Do you remember me carrying you to bed last night?"

She considered lying, but decided that was not a particularly sound basis on which to build a relationship. The truth wasn't going to do her much good, either, but at least she wouldn't be deluding herself. “Yes, I remember bits and pieces.”

“Do you . . . remember what you said to me?”

“Yes.” Her gaze dropped to her mug. “I’m sorry.”

“You’re sorry? Does that mean . . . you didn’t mean it?”

His tone was so hopeful, Sherry wanted to throw something at his thick head. She glanced up, and found hope gleaming in his eyes, too. The clod. “I wish I could tell you what you want to hear, Kit,” she said, “but I can’t. I meant it.”

Plowing his fingers through his hair, he swore under his breath. “God, Sherry.” He shook his head, staring at the floor. “I don’t know what to say.”

Sherry stood up. “You don’t need to say anything. I understand—maybe more than you do—what this means.”

“What does it mean?” he asked, meeting her gaze once more.

“It means that we just engaged in a good old-fashioned one-night stand.”

“What?”

“It means, Mr. Good Time Kit, that the good times between us are over.”

“But why?” He set down his mug and moved to her, taking her shoulders. “I wish I could give you what you want from me. But I can’t. That doesn’t mean we can’t . . . enjoy each other’s company for as long as it lasts.”

Sherry wanted to scream and cry and pound his chest with her fists. But dignity was the only thing she still had going for her, so she laughed instead. “Oh, Kit, you are such a man.”

Pulling her closer, he said, “You didn’t seem to dislike that about me last night.”

“I’m not talking about the physical. I’m talking about the emotional.” She squirmed. “Let me go.”

“Tell me you don’t like being this close to me.”

“I love being this close to you. Too much, in fact. Let me go.”

He didn’t. “Tell me you didn’t enjoy yourself last night.”

Sherry rolled her eyes. “I had a blast. I saw stars. I came as close to heaven as I ever will, I think. Feel better?”

"Then why would you give it up?"

Her heart ached, because she didn't want to. But she didn't have a choice. She needed to cut her losses, before she fell so hard she'd never recover.

In a burst of painful clarity, she had to admit that this situation was not Kit's fault. He'd been honest about his desires and limitations from the very beginning. She'd been the one to lie, to herself and to him. She thought she could handle it. She thought she could take the desire and leave the emotion out of it. But she couldn't. And neither of them deserved a scene sometime in the future, of Sherry clinging to him as he tried to walk away. Of her begging him not to leave her, to love her forever.

"Tell me something, Kit," she said softly. "Have your rules changed at all after last night?"

He looked into her eyes, searching for she didn't know what. But when his taut features seemed to go even tighter in grim resignation, she had her answer before he spoke. "No, Sherry, the rules haven't changed."

She shrugged off his hands and stepped back. "That's all the answer you need, don't you think?"

She started to turn away, but he grasped her upper arm and swung her back to him. In the blink of an eye, he had her in his arms. "You knew the rules last night, Sherry. But still you let me make love to you. What's different today?"

Dignity be damned. "You didn't make love to me, Kit. You had sex with me."

He waved. "Whatever. You still knew the rules."

"You're right. I knew the rules. It's not your fault I can't live with them."

"Why not?"

"Because, you fool, I'm in love with you!"

"Aw, damn," he said, letting her go so fast, you'd think she'd caught fire. He threw back his head, staring at the ceiling. "I'm sorry."

He was sorry. Her heart was shattering, and he was *sorry*. Oh, what an idiot she'd been. "Yeah, well, me too."

"But . . . I'm not ready to let this go, Sherry."

"It's not your choice to make."

"Go out to dinner with me tonight."

"No."

"Lunch."

"No."

"Dammit, why not?"

Sherry folded her arms over her chest. "I have my own set of rules, Kit. And I'm not wasting my time with a man who doesn't have any intention of living by them."

His brow creased. "What rules are those?"

She held up five fingers and started ticking them off. "I want a man who respects me."

"I respect you."

She snorted. "I want a man who knows how to romance me."

"I'm trying to learn!"

"I want a man who makes love to *me*."

He opened his mouth.

"With the emphasis on love."

He shut his mouth with a click.

"I want commitment, marriage, children—the works, Kit."

His face drained of all color and he cleared his throat.

"I want happily ever after," she added for good measure. "I believe in happily ever after, and I'm not settling for anything less."

He rubbed his forehead and swore softly. "Sherry—"

"No!" She held out her hands, warding him off. "No, don't say anything." Turning away, she asked, "Where's the dryer? I'm sure my clothes are ready by now." She began walking toward the door.

"Sherry?"

At the threshold she stopped, but didn't look back. "What?" she whispered, her voice croaky with suppressed tears. She would *not* cry, dammit! At least not in front of him.

"For the record, if I could love a woman that way . . . I'd choose you."

Her throat completely closed at that declaration. A good thing, too. Otherwise she'd break out in hysterical laughter. "What a flatterer you are, Mr. Fleming."

Twelve

"You look great," the male model said, his eyes roaming appreciatively over the female model, who did, indeed, look fantastic. Her shining black hair was arranged in an artless bun, her black lycra dress hugged her curves. Her creamy skin screamed for a man's touch.

"Thank you," she murmured, her color rising alluringly on her cheeks.

"You smell great, too," he added holding out a single white rose.

She said nothing, just took the flower and brought it to her nose.

The man reached out and touched her bare arm. "You even feel great," he said, his voice slightly husky. Then he cleared his throat. "Well, are you ready?"

"Yes, I'm ready," she said, her smile turning provocative.

As the man turned to open the door for her, the woman looked directly into the camera and added, "Thanks, Bella Luna, for making my date."

Sherry clicked off the VCR before all of the technical information came on, then nodded at Kit's secretary, who turned up the lights.

Sherry glanced around the room and found everyone looking to Kit for his reaction. He was staring thoughtfully at the blank screen, his opinion unreadable.

Sherry's heart pumped painfully as she peered at him, as it had the dozen or so times she'd seen him since their night together. He was such a disgustingly handsome beast and he didn't love her. Two perfectly good reasons to hate him. Unfortunately, she couldn't bring herself to do it.

Seeing him today hurt more than usual, though. Because it

would be the last time. After this morning's meeting, Kit Fleming was out of her life for good. Then she could truly set about the business of purging him from her system.

He glanced over at her, and his gaze flickered up and down her body impassively. The jerk. After a couple of half-hearted attempts at asking her out the first few times they'd seen each other after that night, he'd reverted to the old unemotional Kit.

"Well?" she said, a little too sharply. She hated the fact that thoughts of him and their night together had consumed her the last two months, while he treated her as if he wasn't sure he remembered her name.

Kit hated the fact that he couldn't help but remember every minute detail about Sherry Spencer, while she treated him as if she wished she could erase every memory they shared.

Damn, he wished she would have let their relationship proceed in a normal fashion. Maybe then he would have gotten her out of his system by now, and thoughts of her would cease to haunt him. Instead, he'd been granted just a little bit of heaven for just one night and it only made him crave more.

He still wanted her. So much, in fact, he hadn't been able to bring himself to sleep with any of the other women he'd dated since his night with her. He deeply resented her for that, considering celibacy had never held any appeal whatsoever for him. If he could have her just one more time, his problems would be solved. He'd sate this gnawing need for her and be able to move on and get back to his normal way of life.

"Well?" she snapped again, dragging Kit from his self-pity.

He examined her again, hoping against hope the raging desire she inspired in him didn't show in his eyes. "It's good." Too good. What they'd shared together had been too good. Too intense. Too incredible. If she'd felt half of what he did during their lovemaking, no wonder she'd fancied herself in love with him.

Gazing into her eyes, he wondered if she still felt that way. Some awful, selfish part of him hoped so. There was something very satisfying about knowing a woman like Sherry could care that much. He didn't deserve her love, he knew, but still the thought of it thrilled some inner part of him. A part he'd thought long gone, killed by foster parents who'd done everything possible to demonstrate that love didn't exist.

He realized, suddenly, that his pronouncement had opened up the floodgates, and the others sitting around the conference table were all talking at once, registering their approval. The ad *was* good. The whole campaign was good. Already the two commercials that had aired were garnering plenty of attention. Fan mail was pouring in, and sales were up. All thanks to this sprite of a woman who could turn him on wearing a severe black business suit.

I want you again, Sherry. He couldn't help the thought. It pounded in his head, in his chest, and lower. He wanted her. But he couldn't have her. Not without all the other baggage that went along with her. Commitment. Marriage. Children. Surprisingly, he didn't shudder at the thought as he normally would. Which just went to show that his hormones were overruling his common sense.

Reining in his desire, he looked down at his legal pad. Checking off number one on his list—*View and Approve Final TV Ad*—he moved to item number two.

Kit waited a few moments for the group to get their congratulations over with, waited while Sherry moved to her chair. She surprised him by beginning to pack up her briefcase, as if the meeting were over.

"Sit down, Ms. Spencer. We have more items on today's agenda."

She glanced up, her beautiful blue eyes regarding him with something close to distaste. Kit couldn't believe how much her expression wounded him. If she still cared about him, she was doing a fine job of masking it.

"You approve of the commercial?" she asked, still not sitting, and still packing.

"Yes, it's fine. Excellent, in fact."

She nodded . . . and kept right on packing. "Fine. Then I believe this meeting's over."

"No, it's not," he said, through gritted teeth. "I want to talk about a concept for the spring campaign."

"Then I suggest you schedule another meeting. One with whoever is taking over the Bella Luna account."

"Excuse me?" Kit said, over the sudden silence screaming throughout the conference room.

"You heard me."

"You're resigning from the account?"

She studied him blandly. "That's right."

Kit's heart began pounding but he tried to match her bored look for bored look. "May I ask why?"

"You may. But I think you already know the answer, Mr. Fleming. I've kept my commitment to see the initial ad blitz through. This is where it ends."

"This is business, Ms. Spencer. Keep your personal feelings out of it."

That stopped her in her tracks. She examined him as if he were a slimy green bug. "No can do, Mr. Fleming." She made eye contact with each of the other seven men in the room. "Gentlemen, it's been a pleasure working with you."

Kit noticed she didn't glance his way again as she said this. In stunned disbelief he watched her lift her briefcase and move to the door.

Jim Forbes jumped up to follow her.

"Forbes!" Kit barked, stopping the man. Jim turned around. "Sit down," Kit commanded, rising himself. "Start talking concept. I'll see Ms. Spencer out."

Sherry wasn't thrilled by that announcement, if her quickened strides were any indication. With a muffled curse, Kit started after her, catching her as she practically ran past his wide-eyed secretary.

"Sherry, wait," he growled. "Let's talk about this."

She yanked her arm out of his grasp and kept right on marching toward the elevator. She snatched her visitor's badge from the lapel of her suit and dropped it on the guard's desk. "Sherry Spencer, checking out."

Kit kept silent as she jabbed at the elevator button. But as soon as the elevator door whooshed open, he stepped in right behind her. She would have stepped out, but he blocked her way. "No, you don't. We're going to talk."

"We have nothing to say," she said, a small catch to her voice.

The hesitation in her tone told Kit what he wanted to know. She still cared. She might hate his guts, but she still cared, too. He couldn't believe how much the thought raised his hopes. "Don't do this, Sherry," he said, grasping her shoulders. "There's no reason for you to resign the account."

She whacked his hip with her briefcase. "Take your hands off me."

He complied, rubbing his thigh. "Ouch!"

For a split second, concern flashed in her eyes, but she quickly masked it. "There is every reason to resign this account. You are a pompous, arrogant, self-centered control freak. No one in her right mind would willingly continue to work with you. Find yourself another account exec."

"You're resigning because of what happened between us. Admit it."

She opened her mouth as if to argue the point, but then shut it with a click of her teeth. After a moment, she said, "Well, that's part of it."

"What if I said I'll stay away from the meetings? What if I say you work directly with Jim from now on?"

She shook her head, and strands of her hair fell free from her bun. "No. I can't do it."

"Why not?"

The elevator door swung open, and she quickly stepped through. "Sherry Spencer, hitting the road at"—she glanced at her watch—"twelve-forty-four," she said to the guard.

Then she headed for the reception area, Kit hot on her heels. At the front door she said to the receptionist, "Sherry Spencer, out of here."

Desperation seized Kit. They couldn't leave it like this. He couldn't stand the thought of this being his last encounter with her. Wild thoughts flew through his head, thoughts of promises and futures, of dropping to his knees and begging her not to do this to them. But as he followed her to her car, he came to his senses. He'd been the one to do this to them, not she. In fact, he'd been the one to declare that there wasn't, and never would be, a them.

As she fumbled with her keys, the desperation in him died a painful death, to be replaced by a despair that was baffling and overwhelming. Sherry started to open the door, but Kit forced it closed, compelling her to turn to him one final time. "What if I told you I was a fool?"

A small sob sounded in her throat, one that made his heart ache. He'd done this to her, hurt her beyond belief. He didn't deserve her love, a love she'd given so honestly, and that he'd tossed aside with an arrogance and stupidity that made him want to hurt himself. Bad.

"I would agree with you," Sherry choked out. "Among other things."

With soul-wrenching resignation, he dropped his hand from the door and stepped back, giving her her freedom. "I wish you well, Sherry."

Her eyes went misty and she blinked rapidly. Without another word she wrenched open the door and climbed in the car, tossing her briefcase on the passenger seat.

She didn't once look at him as she put the vehicle in gear and drove away.

Kit watched the car until it disappeared from sight. A burning in his chest nearly consumed him, and for a moment he doubled over, propping his hands on slightly bent knees.

His breath was choppy, his throat all but closed. Far, far too late, he understood what had happened.

He was in love. It had taken him thirty-six years, but he'd finally found love. And the woman he loved had just driven out of his life.

Forever.

"Well, sis, you finally got your wish."

Kit took the drink Rachel handed him and dropped glumly

onto the chintz couch in her sitting room.

Rachel quickly joined him, her eyes brimming with alarm. "Kit, you look awful. Like you haven't slept in a week. What's wrong?"

Kit sipped his tonic and lime, feeling every weary muscle in his body start to relax. It had only been four days, actually, since Sherry had zoomed out of his life, but it felt more like four centuries. But Rachel was right. He hadn't slept a wink in that time, too angry over his utter stupidity. And too confused.

Love sucked.

"Kit, you're frightening me!" Rachel said. "Please, tell me what's wrong."

"I'm in love," he stated flatly, glaring at the bubbles in his drink as if they'd been personally responsible for his sorry state. Absolute silence greeted his declaration. When he couldn't stand the screaming shock permeating the room another moment, he looked up and barked, "Well? What do you have to say to that? Your fondest dream has been realized, sister of mine."

"You don't look thrilled," Rachel commented dryly.

"Thrilled?" Kit emitted a gritty burst of laughter. "No, I am not thrilled. Horrified, terrified, maybe, but definitely not thrilled."

Laughing softly, Rachel patted his shoulder. "My condolences."

"This isn't funny."

She did a really lousy job of stifling her smile. "No, of course not."

"It's a nightmare."

"Terrible," Rachel agreed.

"Horrendous."

"Ghastly," she choked out.

"You're laughing at me."

"I most certainly am."

"Well, cut it out."

Rachel set down her own drink and gave Kit a quick, fierce hug. "I'm so happy for you."

Kit growled. "Don't be."

She sat back and peered at him. "Why not? Kit, love isn't a disease. It's something to be treasured."

He stared down into his drink again. "Not if the feeling isn't returned."

"Oh, no," Rachel whispered. "Oh, Kit, I'm sorry."

"She did love me once, but I blew it."

"Is it . . . Sherry?"

"Yes." He rubbed his chest, which hadn't stopped aching for four freaking days. He wasn't certain it would ever stop. How could he have been so blind? So stupid? So incredibly arrogant? For months he'd been somewhat content, secure in the knowledge that a woman like Sherry could love him. Secure in the knowledge that he'd get to see her, if only during business hours.

Yes, he'd missed her, yearned to make love to her again. But incredible fool that he'd been, he'd considered keeping their relationship professional a noble gesture. It had never occurred to him that the thoughts of her that consumed him all these months had been born of love. For that he was paying. Paying dearly.

"Kit, love doesn't just go away," Rachel put in quietly. "If she truly loved you, she most likely still does."

Kit looked up, the vise in his chest easing. "Do you really believe that?"

"Absolutely. Honest love is for keeps."

"You mean," he said, touching his chest again, "this awful feeling is never going away?"

"Never."

"Damn," he muttered. "What the hell am I going to do?"

"Well, for starters, you could try fighting for her."

"Fighting for her," he repeated. "How?"

"By telling her . . . wait a minute, no . . . by *showing* her how you feel."

Setting down his drink, Kit pondered the idea. "Showing her . . ." he mused. He turned to his sister. "You know, I saw this movie once." He waved. "I forget the name, but Cary Grant was in it. He wanted to propose to his woman on top of the

Empire State Building."

"An Affair To Remember."

"Right!" Kit said, pointing at Rachel's nose. "Maybe I could drag her to the Empire State Building and propose."

Rachel smiled. "A grand gesture, to be sure."

Kit's enthusiasm shriveled. "Sherry's not big on grand gestures."

"What's she big on?"

"What do you mean?"

"What does she want, Kit?"

He thought about that. "Commitment. Marriage. Children. The works."

"Are you willing to give her all that?"

A twinge of panic bit into him at the idea of marriage and children. Two things he'd sworn his whole life he would never have. But the panic subsided as fast as it had hit him, and suddenly longing took its place. The thought of commitment to Sherry, marriage, children with her, became the single most appealing idea he'd ever had. He wanted it all, too. He wanted it all . . . with her.

He smiled as he considered Sherry transforming his house into a home to be cherished. A haven filled with love and laughter and kids. Jumping up, he hauled a surprised Rachel to her feet and trapped her in a bear hug. "Have I ever told you I love you, sis?"

Rachel stared up at him, then blinked over suddenly wet blue eyes. "No, Kit, you haven't. But I've always known it."

"A very big mistake on my part. I love you, Rachel."

"I love you, too."

He released her, then grabbed his jacket from the chair where he'd flung it. "Gotta go. I've got a lot of stupidity to make up for."

Sherry let herself into her apartment building tiredly. Every muscle she owned begged for relief. In the last week she'd taken to jogging until she nearly dropped, hoping to clear her head, to ignore her aching heart. It wasn't working. Thoughts of Kit and the fact that she'd never see him again in this lifetime were nearly killing her.

Even from down the hall she saw the small green item taped to her door. She stopped dead for a moment. And then adrenaline pumped into her tired body, and she broke into a run. With shaking hands she pulled the twenty dollar bill from the door and turned it over. And her heart stopped beating.

For a lifetime, call Kit.

Sherry slumped against the doorframe, her heart picking up the beat, pounding in almost painful spurts. Shaking, she let herself into her condo and stopped in the middle of the living room, unsure what to do next. *For a lifetime, call Kit.* What did it mean? And did she want to call and find out?

Of course she did. Didn't she?

Laying the twenty on the coffee table, she decided to ponder it over a nice cool shower. After all, she didn't want to call the man when she was all sweaty and everything. She took two steps toward her bathroom before she swung back and lunged for the phone. Sweat be damned.

Kit answered before she even heard a ring. "Fleming," he said, his voice pitched low.

"Spencer," she answered, in a breathless whisper. Her pulse was threatening to send her into cardiac arrest.

"I wasn't sure you'd call."

"I . . . wasn't sure I should."

"I'm glad you did."

She wanted to be cool and aloof and emotionless. Too bad she didn't have enough willpower to pull it off. His tone, his hesitation, his . . . lack of control snapped her good sense in two. "What does this mean, Kit?"

"Will you come to my house, Sherry? I want to show you something."

"What?"

"I don't want to tell you, I want to show you. Please, Sherry."

"Are you demanding my presence, Mr. Fleming?"

"I'm asking. I'm . . . begging."

"Oh, Kit," she breathed. "I don't want you begging."

"Whatever it takes, I'm willing. Please, Sherry, come over."

"All right," she said slowly. "Can you give me an hour?"

"It'll be the longest damn hour of my life. But yes, of course."

"Can you give me a hint what this is about?"

"I want to show you my new rules."

As fast as she got ready, Sherry could've been at Kit's in half an hour, maybe less. But she forced herself to dawdle at home. Wouldn't do to appear too eager, even though she was buzzing with anticipation.

Was it possible? No, she couldn't believe it. Not until she heard it from the man's sexy lips.

She arrived at Kit's house exactly one hour after the phone call. Fashionably late was not a phrase in her lexicon at the moment. He answered the door before she rang the doorbell. They stared at each other in silence for the longest time. Awareness thrummed through her, as she remembered the last time she'd been here, and what had happened to her then. The way he'd loved and cherished her with his hands, his body . . . and his heart, whether he'd realized it or not.

God, she loved the idiot.

Kit shook his head as if to clear it and stepped back. "Come in."

Sherry blinked, then willed her legs forward. He looked absolutely scrumptious today. His honey-brown hair was still damp at his temples, and his eyes had taken on a forest green hue. He wore a pale green oxford shirt, sleeves rolled, and khaki-colored chinos that hugged his hips lovingly.

Sherry's chest grew warm and tight at the look in Kit's eyes. If he didn't say another word, she'd still know. He cared about her. Really cared. Unfortunately for him, she was going to force him to spell it out.

"Are you going to tell me what this means?" she asked,

pulling the twenty dollar bill from her jeans pocket.

"Yes," he said, but just stood there like a gorgeous lump.

Sherry waited. And waited. "Well?"

He shook his head, chuckling. "I'm just . . . so glad you came. I don't know where to start."

"How about at the beginning?"

"Do you have any idea how much I want you right now?"

She had a pretty good idea. If he wanted her a fraction as much as she wanted him, his pants were probably feeling a bit tight at the moment. Every nerve in her screamed for her to jump into his arms, to kiss him, hold him, love him. But not yet. She wasn't risking her heart again. Not until he risked his.

"That's a moot point, Kit, as long as the rules are still the same."

"Ah, yes, the rules. I'll let you decide. Come with me."

He held out his hand. Sherry hesitated a moment before she laid her palm to his. Kit turned and tugged her toward his formal living room. Throwing open the doors, he pulled her inside.

Sherry gasped as she looked around. The room was completely bare. Not a stitch of furniture or drapes remained. All that was left from the room she remembered was the elaborate wallpaper and wainscoting. "Were you robbed?"

Before she knew it, she was in his arms. He gazed down on her with a half-smile. "Yes, I was. For thirty-six years."

"Wh-what?"

"For thirty-six years I was robbed of so many things. Laughter. Joy." He took a deep breath. "Love."

"Oh, Kit, I—"

He laid a finger on her lips. "Then a few months ago this woman came into my life. And all of a sudden I felt . . . happy. Suddenly smiling was easy. Every time I was with her, I felt . . . good. And I was too blind to realize why."

"What does that have to do with this?" she said, indicating the empty room.

He took her shoulders and turned her to face the vast barrenness. "*This* is me without you. Empty. Lifeless." Swinging her back to him, he looked deep into her eyes, and Sherry was lost. "I need you in my life, Sherry. Without you, I'm just a shell. You fill something in me, and I need that. I need you."

"But—"

"No! Don't say anything yet. Let's complete the tour." He took her hand and led her to the foyer, then to the wide staircase. He took one step and stopped. "Oh, what the hell."

With that he swept her into his arms and Sherry gasped. With a grin, he kissed her. "Even I've seen *Gone With The Wind*."

Sherry thought of what the staircase scene had led to in the classic movie, and heat filled her belly, flashing along her nerve endings. As he ascended the steps, she thought about what she would do if he tried to take her to bed right now. She knew she shouldn't do it, but she wasn't certain she had the strength of will to deny him.

Apparently it didn't matter, because instead of turning right to his bedroom, he turned left at the top of the stairs. At the first guest bedroom he stopped and opened the door.

Sherry gasped again as she looked around. He'd transformed the room from its previous flowery opulence to a . . . nursery.

Kit set her down and silently allowed her to check out the room, with its bright, multicolored clown wallpaper, to the hand-carved crib, changing table, a rocking chair and armoires. Stuffed animals littered the place.

"The rules have changed, Sherry," he finally said quietly. "I want it all with you. Commitment, marriage, children . . . eventually. I want you. Not just to share my bed, but my life. To make this house a home. Only you can do that for me."

Sherry's throat burned with emotion. Her eyes filled with tears. Her heart swelled. She turned to him, then threw herself in his arms. "It took you long enough to realize it, you idiot," she choked out.

Brushing back her hair, he smiled wryly. "Sometimes I'm a little slow on the uptake."

He kissed her. The kiss held the promise of tomorrow, and Sherry felt her soul heal, and her heart fill with an overwhelming love and passion. She twined her arms around his neck and pressed into him, returning the kiss, the promise.

He cupped her face and broke the kiss. "Tell me you'll marry me." Another quick kiss. "I promise, if you'll be my wife, I'll supply you with more chocolate than you could possibly eat. I'll give you romance and love and fidelity and as many children as you want. And," he added, smiling suggestively, "I'll be your slave boy for the rest of our lives."

Sherry choked on her laughter, grabbed his shirt in both fists and pulled him to her. "There's not a woman on earth who'd be dumb enough to refuse an offer like that."

A Funny Thing Happened . . .

Trish Jensen decided to become a romance writer when she learned the rule about romance writers not having to do housework. Really! It's an honest-to-goodness rule! Well, okay, it was the most creative excuse she could come up with when she tried to explain her theory on dustballs to visitors. (Dustballs don't kill, people do.)

In truth, she discovered writing on her way to getting an MBA. The MBA has long been abandoned in favor of a computer and characters she argues with out loud. (The dog has finally stopped looking around the room, wondering who she's talking to.) Trish and her black lab reside in Amish country, the mountains of central Pennsylvania.

CPSIA information can be obtained
at www.ICGtesting.com
Printed in the USA
LVHW112212090919
630533LV00001B/29/P

9 781611 942101